TM

NICKELODEON®

A novelization by
Cathy East Dubowski
and Mark Dubowski

Based on the screenplay
written by David N. Weiss
& J. David Stem

A
MINSTREL®
BOOK

New   ...KS   ...okyo   Singapore

To our own two rugrats, Lauren and Megan,

who made us what we are today—their mom and dad!

A MINSTREL PAPERBACK *Original*

A Minstrel Book published by
POCKET BOOKS, a division of Simon & Schuster Inc.
1230 Avenue of the Americas, New York, NY 10020-1586

ISBN: 0-671-02106-0

First Minstrel Books printing November 1998

10 9 8 7 6 5 4 3

A MINSTREL BOOK and colophon are registered trademarks of Simon & Schuster Inc.

Cover art by Gabor Csupo and Laslo Nosek
Book design and composition by Diane Hobbing of Snap-Haus Graphics

Printed in the U.S.A.

PROLOGUE

Ancient ruins twilight

Well-worn boots stomped along an overgrown trail that led into the heart of the jungle. The gathering darkness twisted the trees and vines into eerie shapes. Birds shrieked overhead.

But nothing could make the small band of adventurers turn back.

The babies were on a quest.

"This place gives me the juice bumps," Chuckie Finster whispered. His already wild red hair stood on end as he shoved his glasses up on his freckled nose and peered into the gloom.

Phil de Ville trembled. "Maybe we should go back . . ."

"Very back!" his twin sister, Lil, added.

The de Ville twins lived next door to the Pickleses on the other side from Tommy. They looked

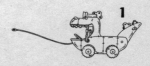

and acted so much the same, people would mistake one for the other. They thought Phil was Lil. Or Lil was Phil. Sometimes Phil and Lil almost got themselves mixed up!

"We can't go back now, you guys!" Tommy Pickles declared. He tugged at the brim of his fedora and shined his flashlight into the darkness. "Okeydokey Jones never goes back. Hang on to your diapies, babies. We're going in!"

"Tommy Pickles," Chuckie whispered with awe, "you're the bravest baby I ever knowed."

Up ahead a massive stone gate guarded the entrance to an ancient temple. Cold air rushed from inside as the gate opened and closed like chomping teeth.

The gaping jaws bore a frightening resemblance to Tommy's three-year-old cousin, Angelica Pickles.

It would have scared the diapers off a normal baby.

Not Tommy Pickles.

He took a slug from his bottle, then hunkered down, waiting to time his leap through the chomping gate.

Phil and Lil crouched side by side, ready to jump in right behind him.

Chuckie was not so brave.

But that was okay. Tommy Pickles and Chuckie

Finster were the bestest friends. So wherever Tommy went, Chuckie followed. They stuck together like peanut butter and jelly.

Tommy grabbed Chuckie's arm and pulled him safely through the perilous jaws.

Inside, a white light shone from the heart of the temple.

Eagerly Tommy led them toward their treasure: a golden object balanced high on an ancient altar.

The babies oohed in awed delight.

Chuckie and the twins strained to lift Tommy toward the treasure. Tommy stretched his arm as far as he could toward their prize. But it was just out of reach.

Would Tommy give up? Never!

Suddenly the ground trembled. The tower of babies wobbled, and Tommy tumbled down.

"Watch out!" Chuckie shouted.

Tommy whirled around. A giant boulder rumbled toward them—bigger than a hundred bowling balls!

Bigger than a thousand bowling balls!

Bigger than all the bowling balls in the world!

The babies screamed and tried to toddle out of the way.

But now a deep, dark pit lay between them and safety.

Tommy and the twins leaped over it, but Chuckie's jump fell short. His fingers clawed the ledge as he began to slide into the pit!

"*Aaarrgh! Yahhh . . . Tommy!*" Chuckie shrieked.

Phil and Lil looked back. The boulder was closing in!

Tommy didn't hesitate. "A baby's gotta do what a baby's gotta do" was his motto. With no thought for his own safety, he charged back to rescue his best friend.

The earth shook.

"C'mon, Chuckie!" Tommy screamed, reaching for his friend's hand.

But it was too late.

A huge dark shadow fell across their terrified faces.

The boulder was about to roll a strike!

There was no escape.

"Tommy!" a woman's voice exclaimed. "You kids shouldn't be playing in here!"

Tommy and his friends blinked and looked around.

The twisted trees and vines melted away. The eerie sounds of jungle creatures died. The ancient temple vanished.

Tommy sighed.

The babies' adventure faded like waking up from naptime.

They were in Tommy Pickles' kitchen.

Instead of entering a tomb, the babies had really climbed into the refrigerator looking for something good to eat. The treasure was really a wedge of golden cake on the middle shelf. The dangerous pit was really a dog bowl, the one that belonged to Tommy's dog, Spike.

And the giant boulder?

That was really Tommy's mom, Didi. Or rather, her great big tummy.

Tommy's mom hadn't always looked like a boulder. He remembered when he could still sit on her lap.

That was a long time ago. Before his mom and dad began to talk about somebody new who was coming to live at their house. Somebody none of them had ever even met before.

Somebody called a sister!

But Tommy wasn't worried.

Tommy liked new things. He liked adventure.

A new sister sounded like an adventure for sure.

But Chuckie was worried. His friends thought the fun times would last forever. . . .

But somehow Chuckie knew.

Everything was about to change.

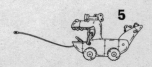

CHAPTER 1

Tommy's mom, Didi, scooped him up, opened the door, and led the children out into the backyard.

Tommy's backyard was just about the best place in the whole wide world. But today it looked even more special.

Tommy looked around in delight. White tables and chairs were set up on the green lawn. Presents towered into the blue sky. Pink ribbons fluttered on the warm afternoon breeze.

Usually the big backyard belonged to Tommy and his friends. But today it was filled with lots of big people. Tommy couldn't understand anything big people said. Neither could his friends. But he understood some things about them, like when they smiled. All the big people in Tommy's yard that day were smiling big.

6

It kind of looked like some great big birthday party.

Hey, thought Tommy. *Maybe it's my new sister's birthday!*

Eagerly he searched the crowd. But he didn't see any new little babies. Only people he knew. Most of them big and old.

There was Chuckie's redhead dad, Charles Senior, otherwise known as Chas. Phil and Lil's parents, Howard and Betty. Cousin Angelica and her dad, Drew, who was also Tommy's uncle. Aunt Miriam. Grandpa Lou. And Grandma Minka and Grandpa Boris.

Tommy waved to his neighbor, three-year-old Susie Carmichael, and her father, Randy.

"Thank you for inviting me to your baby shower, Mrs. Pickles," Susie said politely. Susie really knew how to make the big people smile.

"Glad you could be here," Didi replied.

"They got anything good to eat in this dump?" Angelica Pickles griped.

"There you are, Didila!" Grandma Minka said. "Come!"

Minka took her grown-up daughter by the hand and led her through the crowd.

"Look what we got for you. Boris, move your *tuchas!*" *Tuchas* meant "behind."

Didi's eyes widened in surprise. Her father,

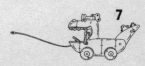

Boris, was holding a present. Or rather, he was holding the leash that went around the present's neck.

"A goat?" Didi choked out. She didn't know what to say. So she said the nice thing people say when they get a present. "Oh, Mom. You shouldn't have."

But this time she really meant it. *Mom, you really, really shouldn't have,* she thought. She gently pushed Tommy behind her. Away from the goat.

Grandma Minka just laughed and patted her daughter's stomach. "Nothing better for little *bubbala* than goat's milk."

"Except maybe yak," Grandpa Boris corrected her. "But you try finding good yak these days!"

Tommy looked at the goat as if he had never seen anything like it before. That's because he hadn't.

Foot by foot, inch by inch, the babies crept toward the strange creature.

BLE-EEE-EEE-EET!

Tommy and his friends jumped away!

Grandpa Boris laughed. "He's saying hello!" He reached into his pocket and pulled out some foil-covered chocolate coins. "Here you go, *kinderlach,*" he said. *Kinderlach* was Grandpa Boris' word for "kids."

The goat was quickly forgotten as Tommy and

his friends reached for the shiny coins. They crawled under one of the pretty white tables to peel off the foil and eat the chocolate hidden inside. Spike, Tommy's faithful dog, came and helped lick the chocolate off their faces.

At last there was only one shiny coin left.

Tommy admired it.

"Are you gonna eat it, Tommy?" Phil asked.

Tommy wanted to. He loved chocolate more than just about anything in the whole world. But he had a better idea.

"Nope," he announced to his friends. "I'm saving it—for my baby sister."

Chuckie pushed his glasses up on his nose and looked around. "You mean she finally came?"

Tommy shook his head. "Not yet. But they're givin' her this big party, so I'm pretty sure today's the day!"

"Do ya think she got losted on her way to the party?" Phil wondered.

Tommy hadn't thought of that. His mom said she would be really little when she came. What if she didn't know their address?

"I don't know," Tommy said with a worried frown. "Maybe we'd better go look for her." He jumped to his feet and hiked up his diaper. "C'mon!"

Like a true brave explorer, Tommy led the way.

Phil and Lil, as always, toddled after him without question.

"Uh, uh, but Tommy!" Chuckie stammered, trying to catch up. "She could be anywheres!"

Didi was chatting with Betty and Aunt Miriam when Angelica's mom, Charlotte, arrived at the party dressed in her blue power suit, her blond hair slicked back into a high sleek ponytail, and talking on her cell phone. She took her phone everywhere.

"I'll get back to you, Jonathan," she said into her phone. "I've got to say hi to the life of the party." She clicked off and thumped Didi's bulging tummy. "How's our little man?"

"I told you, Charlotte," Didi reminded her. "Dr. Lipschitz says it's a girl."

"Ha!" Betty roared. "That windbag thought Phil and Lil were intestinal gas!"

Aunt Miriam nodded her head. She agreed with Betty and Charlotte. As proof the expected baby was a boy, she quoted an old saying about the shape of a mother's tummy. "Ridin' high, it's a guy!"

Charlotte started to chime in with her own old saying, too. "You know what they say—"

Ring!

For once in her life, Didi was glad when

Charlotte's cell phone rang and interrupted the conversation.

"Now, now," Didi said to the others. "Dr. Lipschitz is the expert. I don't see any of you with a Ph.D. in Latin."

"Yeah, Pig Latin, maybe!" Betty joked. "Well, let's just hope for Tommy's sake it's a girl. I'd hate to think how much my pups would be squabblin' if they were both boys."

"Uh-uh-uh!" Didi said politely, wagging her finger. She made it a point to read every book she could find about raising children. And she tried hard to do everything the experts—especially Dr. Lipschitz—advised. "Let's not do any gender stereotyping. After all, Stu and Drew are brothers. And they get along just fine."

"Lazy—"

"Pushy—"

"Inconsiderate—"

"Bossy—"

"Why can't you listen to me?"

"Why can't you listen to *me?*"

At the moment, brothers Stu and Drew Pickles were not getting along just fine.

They were down in Stu's basement, arguing like kids on the playground.

Grandpa Lou leaned back in his chair, tinkering

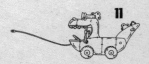

with his pocket watch. His bushy gray mustache twitched as he chuckled over his two sons. *Those rascals!* He could remember their very first squabble. It was over a pacifier. He couldn't remember who won that one. But it seemed like those boys had been wrasslin' with each other over something ever since.

"You two are noisier than a pair of polecats in mating season!" Grandpa Lou told them.

But Stu and Drew were not really a "pair" of anything. They were exact opposites. East and west. Summer and winter. Candy and vegetables.

Angelica's dad, Drew Pickles, was a by-the-book kind of guy. Clean-cut, with sensible glasses and neatly combed hair. He liked to wear sweater-vests and plain, neat ties.

He'd made a good career for himself as an investment banker. He liked the way cold hard numbers lined up in neat rows and columns. He liked the way two plus two always added up to four, come rain or shine, winter, summer, spring, or fall. He liked things neat and in order. Safe and sound.

As a kid, he always colored inside the lines.

Tommy's dad, Stu Pickles, lived his whole life outside the lines.

He had wild hair, his clothes often looked as if he'd worn them for days, and he favored loud polka-dot ties. Stu liked dreaming. In the morning he didn't go off to work. He went down into the basement. From there he ran his own business—Pickles Industries. He was a toy inventor.

That drove Drew crazy.

Stu shoved his welder's mask down over his face and went back to work. Sparks showered the room as he welded another piece onto his latest invention.

This was the one. The one that was finally going to make him rich.

Drew just couldn't understand his little brother. He thought Stu needed to grow up and take more responsibility for his family. He thought Stu was too big to play with toys.

Ever since he'd heard about the new baby on the way, he'd tried to talk Stu into finding a more responsible way to earn a living. "We're talking about a real job, Stu," Drew tried one more time. "With benefits."

Stu flipped his mask back up. "Hey, I'm not gonna waste my life as a clock-punching, paper-pushing, bean-counting—"

He broke off as he saw his brother frown. After all, that was exactly what Drew was. "Uh . . . uh no offense."

Drew threw up his hands. "You barely make ends meet now," he said. "You've got no insurance,

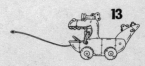

no savings—and another kid on the way."

Stu shut off his welding iron and smiled at his big brother. "For your information, bro, I am working on something right now that is going to put this branch of the Pickles family on Easy Street."

"What is it this time, huh?" Drew shot back. "An electric sponge?"

"Of course not!" Stu replied indignantly. "That was last year."

He stepped aside, waving his arm at his latest invention.

It looked like the punch line to the joke: "What do you get when you cross a dinosaur with a baby stroller?"

Inside the dinosaur's gaping mouth was a seat and a steering wheel.

"This," Stu announced dramatically, "is the Reptar Wagon. The ultimate in twenty-first century toddler transportation." He took a deep breath and sighed with pride. "The perfect children's toy."

Stu had named his invention after the famous movie star and dinosaur Reptar. His son Tommy and all his friends were crazy about Reptar. Stu figured his Reptar Wagon would be a big hit, too.

Grandpa Lou grunted. "In my day we had plenty of fun just throwing rocks at each other.

Big bag of dirt clods! That's what kids want."

For once, Stu and Drew did something the same. They both rolled their eyes at their father's story about how tough things were in "the old days."

Stu turned to his workbench, searching among the junk. At last he found it—a newspaper. He held it open to a full-page ad for his brother to see.

It showed a picture of a man named Mr. Yamaguchi posed outside his corporate offices.

"The Reptar Corporation is holding a toy design contest," Stu revealed. "And the winner gets five hundred dollars—"

"Oooooh!" Drew teased.

Stu ignored his brother. "And," he added, "there'll be plenty more if this toy's a hit. And I'll be famous—"

"Oh, yeah, yeah, yeah," Drew said, shaking his head. "That's what you said when you built *that* stupid thing." He pointed to the ceiling.

A huge metal pterodactyl dangled from the ceiling. Handlebars and pedals hung beneath it. If a person got on and pedaled the contraption like a bike, it was supposed to make the pterodactyl fly like a small plane.

Stu shrugged. "Okay, so maybe Dactar was a little complex," he admitted. "But this . . . this . . ."

Words seemed to fail him. So he picked up a small microphone and grinned. "Watch."

Softly he spoke into the mike: "I am Reptar, hear me roar."

Instantly the words were translated by a computer chip, and a terrifying voice roared from the Reptar Wagon:

"I AM REPTAR! HEAR ME ROAR!!!"

Drew and Grandpa jumped.

Giggling, Stu pressed another button.

Fffffffffft!

Flames burst from Reptar's mouth!

It was quite a sight.

Especially when it set the newspaper ad and part of the basement on fire.

With a shriek, Stu quickly stomped out the flames.

"Conflabbit!" Grandpa Lou hollered, leaping up from his chair. "Can't a man work in his own basement without gettin' barbecued?"

Stu blushed. "Okay, so maybe *real* fire isn't the best idea for a children's toy."

Drew snickered and stared at the ceiling. "What a nincompoop!"

"Hey, don't you have some beans to count somewhere?"

"Nincompoop!" Drew said again.

"Bean counter!"

"Nincompoop!"

"Bean counter!"

Grandpa Lou jumped between them. "Will you two grow up?"

Stu and Drew hung their heads like scolded ten-year-olds.

"Sorry, Pop," they mumbled at the same time.

Grandpa Lou nodded. He knew that despite the way they acted sometimes, his sons really loved each other. Satisfied, he headed toward the stairs.

"Nincompoop!" Drew whispered behind his father's back.

"Bean counter!" Stu whispered right back.

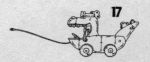

CHAPTER 2

Where does a baby look for a new baby sister?

Tommy thought way, way back to when he was really little. Back then, he remembered, he'd spent most of his time in his warm, cozy crib. Maybe that's where his baby sister would be.

Tommy and his friends crept into his room to see.

Phil and Lil gasped. Chuckie nearly dropped his glasses.

They looked around Tommy's room, not believing their eyes.

Once upon a time the walls of Tommy's room were painted blue. His crib sat right in the middle. The whole room had belonged to him!

Now everything looked different.

"Tommy!" Chuckie exclaimed. "Somebody's

been coloring your room!"

Tommy nodded. Now half the room was painted . . . pink!

"Yep," he said with a proud smile. "It's for my new sister."

The kids couldn't help but notice that there was another bed in the room, too.

A grown-up bed.

Tommy didn't understand the squiggles painted on the headboard. But his mom had told him they were letters. Letters that spelled "Tommy."

His mom had told him that soon his baby sister would come, and that she would sleep in his crib. Tommy would get to move into the grown-up "Tommy" bed.

At first Tommy was a little worried. How could he leave the snugly security of the only bed he'd ever known? The new bed seemed as big as a mountain. And it smelled funny.

But his mom seemed so happy about it. So Tommy figured he'd give it a try.

And besides, it would be nice to have somebody in the same room with him at night.

Tommy took a few steps toward the bed. *Hey, neat!* Today the bed had a huge mound of cookies and other goodies piled right in the middle.

Maybe his mom was trying to help him like his new bed.

But Tommy couldn't think about that right now. He had to find his new sister.

Tommy and his friends searched the room. They looked in every corner. Inside the closet. Behind the door.

But his new baby sister wasn't there. Not even hiding under the blankets in his crib.

"How are we gonna find her, Tommy?" Phil asked.

"Yeah," Chuckie worried. "We don't even know what she looks like."

"Well, she's a girl, like me," Lil pointed out. She patted her blue dress with the yellow ducky sewn on it. "So we know she'll be prettyful."

Just then a small hurricane—also known as Angelica Pickles—blew into the room.

"Out of my way, you dumb babies!" she hollered. She clutched the hem of her purple dress out in front of her, making a basket out of the skirt.

It was filled with cookies!

Tommy's cousin Angelica was a bossy, smarty-pants know-it-all. Her favorite sport was telling Tommy and his friends what to do. That and eating cookies.

Angelica stomped over to the new bed as if she owned the place and dumped the cookies on the pile.

So *that's* where all the goodies came from.

Angelica tossed a scornful look at the babies. "I gotta get back to the dessert table afore the growed-ups eat all the good stuff."

Hey, Tommy thought. Angelica was four years old. She'd been around the block. And she knew a whole bunch more than babies did about what went on in the grown-up world.

Maybe this was one of those times when a bossy, smarty-pants know-it-all might actually come in handy.

"Angelica," Tommy asked, "can you help us find my baby sister?"

Angelica stopped and slowly turned around. Her eyes narrowed to tiny slits, and a sly grin sliced across her face.

"I wouldn't be in such a big hurry if I was you, Tommy," she warned.

"Huh?"

Angelica chuckled knowingly. "'Cause when the new baby gets here, she's gonna get all the toys and the love and the attentions, and your mommy and daddy'll forget all about you. It'll be like . . ."

How could she explain? Of course!

She glared at Cynthia. Cynthia was Angelica's fashion doll. She had a dazed expression that Angelica liked, and half her hair was missing, which Angelica didn't mind at all. Angelica pretended she was Tommy's dad and Cynthia was Tommy's mom. "Look, Didi," Angelica said in a deep voice, "there's that little *bald* kid in the house again."

"My mommy and daddy won't forget me!" Tommy protested.

Angelica laughed scornfully. "That's what Spike said. Before you were born. Back when his name was . . . Paul."

The babies stared at Spike.

The dog chewed at his shoulder, trying to get rid of a flea.

"Paul?" Tommy said in disbelief.

"Yeah," Angelica snapped. "But then you came along, and they put him out in the rain—and he turned into a dog!"

The babies gasped.

"That's not going to happen to me, Angelica!" Tommy insisted. *Angelica knows just about everything,* he thought. *But this time she's just plain wrong.* "My mommy and daddy'll love me no matter what."

But Angelica wasn't even listening anymore.

Something new had caught her eye—something more interesting than a bunch of dumb babies. She ran to the window to look out into the backyard.

Her neighbor and arch rival, three-year-old Susie Carmichael, stood in the middle of the yard. She was singing at the top of her voice. And she was surrounded by adoring grown-ups!

Hey, that's my job! Angelica thought. *How dare she!*

"Who does Susie Carmichael think she is?" Angelica exclaimed, jamming her fists on her hips. Outraged, she stomped outside.

In the backyard, Angelica found Susie singing a song called "A Baby Is a Gift from Above."

Except Susie had misunderstood the words a little. She thought the words were "A Baby Is a Gift from a Bob."

Tommy and his friends toddled out into the backyard just in time to hear the last verse.

"Do you really think babies are a gift from a Bob?" Chuckie whispered to Tommy.

"I don't know," Tommy said. "Why?"

"'Cause," Chuckie said. He pointed to a table overflowing with pink-wrapped baby gifts. "If Bob bringed a gift, maybe your sister's in one of those boxes."

Tommy's eyes lit up. He hadn't thought of that!

All the grown-ups were busy watching Susie and Angelica. There was no one to tell Tommy and his pals to "be careful," or "go that way," or "don't open the gifts."

Tommy grabbed one and *riiiip!* He looked inside.

No baby. Just a tiny pink hat and sweater.

Riiip! No baby. Just some pants. Swimming pants? They were made out of rubber. . . .

Riiip! Wheeee! This was fun!

Tommy ripped into present after present. The pile of paper and ribbon grew higher and higher around them.

No baby in this box. Or this box. Or this box.

But Tommy wasn't a quitter. He wouldn't stop looking till he'd opened every single gift.

Just as he reached for the last box, he heard Susie sing the last line of the song.

Interrupted by Angelica singing her own last word even louder.

All the grown-ups smiled and clapped.

All of them except Didi Pickles.

She sat up suddenly, clutching her tummy. Her eyes widened behind her round green glasses. Her mouth formed a little O of surprise.

Her tummy felt weird.

Really weird—like the day Tommy was born.

Didi reached out and grabbed her friend Betty by the sleeve of her lavender sweatshirt. "Betty . . ." Didi said, her voice a mixture of nervousness and excitement, "it's time!"

Time for what? Betty started to say. *Time to open the presents? Or another jar of pickles?*

But then she saw the look on her best friend's face. That funny look of surprise that all mothers got when "Someday . . ." turned into—

"RIGHT NOW!"

No doubt about it.

It was time for the baby!

Tommy's little sister was on the way!

"It's time!" Betty bellowed. Her loud voice boomed across the yard as she began to bark orders like a drill sergeant. "Everybody to your stations, people! Howard—get Stu! Charlotte—call the hospital! Didi—start your breathing! Come on, good girl!"

Together she helped Didi begin the breathing exercises for new mommies that Dr. Lipschitz taught her.

"Hee hee foo! Hee hee foo! Hee hee foo!"

"Good girl!" Betty coached.

Tommy and his friends shoved aside the piles of gift wrap and looked around to see what was happening.

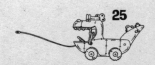

All the grown-ups who were not having babies began running around waving their arms and shouting.

Tommy laughed. Was this some kind of birthday game?

The noise frightened Grandpa Boris' goat. It began to buck and kick.

Its strong hooves knocked over a table of food.

The table hit a sprinkler valve, and the lawn sprinklers gushed up from the ground. The grown-ups shrieked and scurried for cover as the water rained down on the party.

Grandpa Lou chuckled and shook his head. "Now, *that's* what I call a baby shower!"

CHAPTER 3

Tommy looked up from his stroller at the stone statue decorating the entrance to the hospital.

The statue was of Dr. Lipschitz. Tommy liked the little stone babies with wings that flew around him.

I guess my baby sister's here somewhere, Tommy figured.

It made sense. The whole party had moved here, along with his mom and dad. The twins' parents, Betty and Howard. Chuckie's dad, Chas.

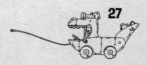

Angelica's parents, Charlotte and Drew. And all the babies in their strollers.

Electric doors swung open as Stu guided Didi into the lobby in a wheelchair. Everyone trooped in behind them like a big parade. A Mother's Day parade.

A nurse dressed in white from head to toe greeted them, then quickly checked her clipboard. "Oh, Mrs. Pickles. You weren't due till next week now, dear." She clucked her tongue. "Well, I guess we could try to squeeze you in somewhere, huh?"

Didi exchanged a look with Stu as he helped the nurse move her onto a rolling metal hospital cart. The doctor arrived—Susie's mom, Dr. Lucy Carmichael. She started to roll the cart away, but Didi put her hand on the doctor's sleeve. Dr. Carmichael stopped the cart with a question in her eyes.

Grandpa Lou knew what was up. He wheeled Tommy's stroller closer to his mother so the boy could tell his mom good-bye.

Didi smiled and stroked Tommy's cheek. "Don't worry, sweetie," she said softly. "Mommy's going to be okay—"

Suddenly she frowned and clutched her tummy. With Stu at her side, Dr. Carmichael whisked the expectant mother away.

Tommy watched them go. Was his mom okay?

"Oh, gosh, Tommy," Chuckie whispered. "Your mommy sure seems upset."

"Maybe your baby sister really is losted," Lil suggested.

Tommy reached into the waistband of his diaper and pulled out the foil-covered chocolate coin that he'd saved. "Well," he said, taking command of the situation. "Maybe we can buy a new one."

Chuckie moaned and spread his hands in the air. "Where are we gonna find a baby in a place like this?"

Tommy glanced left and right. One thing was for sure: This was not a time to stand and wait. Even if they *were* standing in the waiting room.

This was a time for action.

Lucky for them, Grandpa Lou and Grandpa Boris were supposed to be watching them. And when grandpas got together, you could count on one thing: They always started talking about "the old days."

So Grandpa Lou and Grandpa Boris didn't notice when the babies crawled out of their strollers and toddled off down the hall.

There was only one problem.

All the hallways looked alike. They seemed to go on forever.

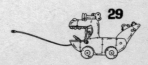

29

All the doors were closed. And all the door-knobs were up where only grown-ups could reach.

This was a tough place for babies!

But would Okeydokey Jones lose hope?

Nope!

Tommy was sure of that. And so the tiny dia-pered search party forged ahead, toddling down the twisting hallways.

Suddenly Tommy stopped in his tracks and shushed his friends.

What was that sound?

Tommy listened closely. It was coming through the wall.

Crying!

Tommy and his friends stood on tiptoe and peeked through a huge glass window.

They gasped when they saw what was inside.

Oh, boy!

And oh, *girl!*

They'd hit the jackpot.

The room was *full* of babies!

"A baby store!" Lil exclaimed.

The kids jumped when the door from the nursery swung open and a nurse rushed out.

Tommy held up his chocolate coin to pay the nurse for a baby.

But the nurse was too busy reading a clipboard

as she hurried past. She didn't even notice the little ones clustered by the door.

Tommy shrugged. He caught the door before it closed, then led his friends inside.

"Mmm," Phil murmured, glancing around at all the newborn babies. "Nice and wrinkly."

Tommy didn't know what to do. Picking a baby was like picking from a box of chocolates: How did you know which one was a good one? What if he picked the one that was all yucky inside?

"You guys," he begged, "help me pick one my mom will like."

Eagerly Tommy and his friends moved from one baby to the next.

They were all so tiny.

And all so pretty.

How could anyone pick just one . . .

Suddenly the door banged open. "There you are!" Grandpa Lou hollered, rushing into the room.

"*Oy!*" Grandpa Boris exclaimed, clutching his heart. "You kids gave my ticker such a scare!"

The grandpas scooped up Tommy and his friends and carried them out the door.

Tommy looked back over Grandpa Lou's shoulder as the baby store got farther and farther away.

Now how am I going to get a baby for my mom? Tommy wondered.

Tommy didn't know it, but his mom didn't need any help finding a baby. In one of the rooms down the hall she had done a fine job of bringing his new baby sister into the world.

The baby looked around at its brand-new world, startled and confused. Then it made a tiny cry.

"Oh, Deed!" Stu gushed. "She's so beautiful! She's so precious! She's—"

Stu's stubbled jaw dropped. He peered more closely at his new baby girl.

And gasped.

He couldn't *believe* what he saw!

Stu Pickles stared at his new baby.

Then he stared at his wife in astonishment. "She's . . . she's . . ." He gulped. "She's a boy!"

Didi smiled as if she had known it all along. She reached out and took the baby into her arms. "Hello, my wonderful sweet baby boy," she cooed.

"Well," Stu said, running a shaky hand through his rumpled purple hair, "I guess we won't be naming him after my mother."

Didi nodded her agreement. "He doesn't look much like a Trixie. . . ." She thought a moment, gazing at the baby's round pink face. "What about my cousin Dylan?"

Hmm, that could work, Stu thought. He tried it out by speaking it aloud to the nurse. "Dylan Prescott Pickles."

"Dil Pickles?" the nurse repeated. She scribbled the name down on her clipboard.

It was official.

"Yeah," Stu murmured happily. "I like it."

Tommy rode high in his Grandpa Lou's arms.

Where were they going?

At last they came to a room, and Grandpa Lou stepped inside.

The room was filled with family and friends and so many flowers it looked like a garden. Everyone stopped talking and stared at Tommy with funny smiles.

Tommy smiled back, then looked around. *Where's my mommy?*

There she is! Tommy sighed in relief.

His mom sat up in a great big bed with lots of pillows tucked all around her. She was smiling now and wearing a pretty new nightgown.

And she was holding a tiny bundle in her arms.

What could it be?

"Well, here you go, sprout," Grandpa Lou whispered.

33

Tommy peered down at the tiny bundle. A wrinkled pink face peeked out.

A baby! Tommy thought. *A tiny baby!*

Was this *their* baby? The one they were going to keep?

He glanced at his mom. She was really smiling now.

Looks like she's happy with this one, he thought.

That was good enough for Tommy. Grinning, he handed Dr. Carmichael his foil-covered chocolate coin. He didn't know how much babies cost. He hoped that would be enough.

Dr. Carmichael's eyebrows shot up. She seemed puzzled. Then she smiled and slipped the coin into her pocket.

Grandpa Lou set Tommy down on Didi's bed, next to his mom and the new baby.

"Tommy," Didi said gently, "I want you to meet someone very special. This is your brother, Dylan. Dil, this is Tommy."

Tommy smiled.

"See?" Didi whispered happily to Betty. "They already love each other."

Dil grabbed Tommy's nose and pulled.

"OWWW!" Tommy cried.

CHAPTER 4

"**W**AAAAAAAAHHHHHHH!"

Baby Dil Pickles was only a month old. But already he had developed a very bad habit.

He cried. A lot. Like, *all* the time.

He cried when he was hungry.

When his diapers were wet.

And sometimes . . . just because.

Of course, Tommy was no stranger to tears. He was a baby, after all. And a baby's world was sometimes filled with heartache: skinned knees; bumps and falls; and ice cream scoops that tumbled from their cones after just one lick and melted on a hot summer sidewalk.

But Dil's crying went beyond normal baby stuff. Tommy's new brother cried day and night.

"Deed, what are we going to do?" Stu wailed

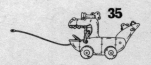

one morning. He paced back and forth with Dil in his arms. "He hasn't stopped crying since we brought him home."

Didi's answer was lost in a big yawn.

Tommy and his friends stared through the bars of their playpen.

"Somehow," Phil griped, "it's not as much fun around here anymore."

"Yeah," Chuckie said uneasily. "What's your brother so sad about, Tommy?"

Tommy shrugged helplessly. "I dunno. But whatever it is, it must be really bad."

"Maybe he's broked!" Lil suggested.

"Broked?" Tommy shook his head and defended his only brother. "He's not broked. He's, uhhh . . . just a little loud."

His friends gave him a doubtful look.

Tommy watched his father wearing circles in the rug as he tried to stop the baby from crying.

"For the love of Pete," Stu asked, "what do you want from us? What? *What?*"

Didi followed her husband around in circles as she flipped through one of her baby books. It was a baby book by Dr. Lipschitz. The purpose of the book was to turn every parent into something Dr. Lipschitz called the "good enough" parent. Stu and Didi felt they weren't there yet, even though they'd read the book cover to cover.

"Oh, there must be something in here we missed," Didi fretted. "Somewhere . . . some-how . . . something."

"There must be. Let me see." Stu continued to jiggle the baby in his arms as he took the book from Didi. "Cats, Colic, Creole baby food . . . Oh, yeah, here it is: Crying." He quickly read the entire section.

The advice was pretty technical. Stu had a hard time understanding it all, he was so sleepy.

But he got Dr. Lipschitz's basic message.

Number one: "The good-enough parent gives up his or her own needs and puts the baby's needs first."

And number two: "When the baby cries, it means you're doing something wrong!"

Tommy looked through the playpen at his dad and his brother.

Dil was still crying.

Now, how come his dad was crying, too?

TOOO-ooo-TOOT! In another part of town a three-car circus train chugged into the station and screeched to a stop.

Two tired-looking clowns jumped down from the cab of the engine and brushed the dust from their clothes.

They were irritated by the sound of the monkeys

chittering nonstop in the third car.

"Serge," one clown said in a thick Russian accent. "You stay here and watch the monkeys. I get us coffee."

A scowl showed through Serge's happy-face makeup. "No, Igor. You stay here and watch the monkeys and I get coffee."

"No. You stay," growled Igor.

"No. You stay!" barked Serge.

"No, you—"

"No, you—"

A few minutes later both clowns went into the coffee shop across the street. They sat at a small table by the front window, where they could drink their coffee and still keep an eye on the train.

Serge grunted. "I think the coffee is better in St. Petersburg." Then he bit into a chocolate doughnut.

"No," Igor insisted, wiping chocolate icing and face paint from his lips. "Is better in Kiev."

"St. Petersburg!"

"Kiev!"

Across the street the train began to move.

Serge bit into another doughnut and stared out the window.

He watched as the train slowly pulled away. . . .
What?

Serge's eyes popped open. He nearly choked.

The train was pulling away!

"Look!" he gasped, grabbing his partner by the arm.

Igor stared in shock.

Instantly they spit out their food and stumbled toward the door like a couple of clowns, knocking over tables, upsetting customers and cups of coffee, and getting tangled in their costumes.

By the time they managed to get outside, it was too late.

The train had disappeared down the tracks.

Serge and Igor hollered and blamed each other in Russian. They slammed their clown hats onto the ground. They stomped their feet.

"Who's driving the train?" Igor wanted to know.

Serge rolled his eyes. He knew—it was as plain as the rubber nose on his face. "I told you to watch the monkeys!" he hollered.

How was I supposed to know monkeys could drive trains? Igor thought. He looked skyward with open arms as Serge smacked him over and over with his floppy hat.

A crowd of passengers getting off another train stopped to clap and cheer. It wasn't every day you got to see a clown act for free.

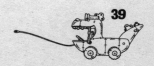

That night Tommy Pickles snuggled up against his mom in his new Tommy bed.

He wasn't all the way used to it yet. But it was great for bedtime stories. Unlike his crib, this bed had plenty of room for his mom to climb in beside him.

As his mom read him a story, Tommy's dad walked up and down the hall just outside the room with Dil on his shoulder.

Dil had the hiccups.

Tommy tried not to let them interrupt the story. He loved this story.

"And then the wizard looked down at the little boy," Didi read aloud, "and said, 'Your wish has been granted.'"

Tommy smiled. He liked that part.

Didi glanced nervously into the hall and turned the page. "And the little boy looked up—"

Stu coughed.

"Waaaaahhhh!!"

"Deed!" Stu cried. "Help!"

Didi sighed and laid the book aside. She gave Tommy a quick hug. "I'll be right back, sweetie."

Tommy's heart sank as his mom got up to help take care of Dil. His mom hadn't made it all the way through a single bedtime story in weeks.

Not since Baby Dil came to live with them.

"All I did was cough, Deed!" Stu said defensively. "I tried not to, but I had a feeling in my throat and then I coughed and now he's crying and he's got the hiccups . . ."

And then Stu totally lost it. He started to cry like a baby.

"Oh, Stu . . ." Didi sighed and stuffed a pacifier in his mouth. Sometimes she felt as if she had three babies in the house!

She wound the mobile over Dil's crib one more time. Stu laid Dil down in the crib and tucked a blanket up to his chin.

The mobile's music box began to play a sweet lullaby.

"Stu . . ." Didi said.

"Yeah?"

"Why don't you sing Dil a lullaby?" she said.

"I'm too tired to sing," he replied.

"All right, I'll make something up," she said.

Stu and Didi took turns making up words to a lullaby as they tried to calm Dil down.

"That was good," Stu said softly as Dil's hiccups faded away.

Now Stu and Didi watched their new baby do something beautiful.

He fell asleep.

The mobile over the crib played out the last few notes of the lullaby.

Stu slipped an arm around Didi's shoulders and sighed. Ahhh. Peace and quiet.

Now everyone was happy.

Almost everyone.

Stu and Didi had both forgotten about Tommy. They had been too busy with Dil to notice when Tommy got up out of his big new bed and crawled into the closet.

As tears filled his eyes, he curled up in the corner with one of his father's fuzzy animal slippers.

Scratching at the back door, forgotten by everyone, Spike the dog howled mournfully into the night.

CHAPTER 5

The next morning Tommy and his friends found a fun new toy to play with in the Pickleses' den.

A big wooden crate.

It was addressed to Mr. Yamaguchi at the Reptar Corporation. It had Stu Pickles' Reptar Wagon inside. He was mailing it to Japan to enter it in Mr. Yamaguchi's toy design contest.

But, of course, the babies couldn't read the mailing address. They just thought it was something new to climb on.

"Hey, sprouts!" Grandpa Lou said, dashing into the room. "A crate's no place for you to play.

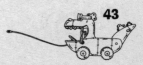

Heh, heh. You wouldn't want to get shipped to Japan with Reptar, now, would you?" He chuckled as he helped Tommy down, then rubbed his scratchy chin. "Hmmm," he muttered to himself. "I better put this where I can keep an eye on it."

Hey, Tommy thought, suprised. *Why is Grandpa Lou dragging our new toy away? Aw, poo.*

That happened a lot with grown-ups. They were always taking fun things away.

Now what?

He and his friends looked around for something else to play with.

Nearby Baby Dil sat in his bouncy chair, clutching a teddy bear and some of his other toys.

Hey! Wait a minute. Those aren't Dil's things. They're my things! Tommy thought.

"Dil!" Chuckie scolded. "That's Tommy's blankey!"

"Yeah," Tommy said. "It used to sleep with me before we even got you." He reached out to take his blanket back.

Whack! Dil socked Tommy with his rattle.

"Ow!" Tommy cried.

"*My* blankey," Baby Dil gurgled. "Thpppt!"

"He's not very nice," Chuckie whispered to Tommy.

Whack!

"Ow!" Chuckie moaned.

Lil planted her fists on her hips and frowned. Neither Tommy nor Chuckie had ever had a brother before. But Lil had. *She* knew about brothers. Tommy was going about it all wrong.

She pulled her friend aside to give him some advice. "That's *not* how you get things from a brother, Tommy."

He rubbed his nearly bald head. "It's not?"

"No, it's not. Here, watch."

Lil toddled over to her twin brother. She smiled into his almost identical face.

And grabbed his Reptar doll.

Phil was surprised, but not enough to let go. "Hey, that's *my* Reptar, Lillian!" He yanked back.

"Is not, Phillip."

"Is, too, Lillian."

"Is not!"

"Is, too!"

This was war.

Tug-of-war!

Phil and Lil dug in their heels. They struggled. They yelled.

But they were perfectly matched in strength. Neither twin could wrench the Reptar toy away from the other.

But Lil had a secret weapon. Right in the middle of the tug-of-war, she did something totally unexpected.

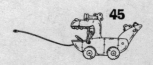

She let go.

Phil went flying backward across the playpen.

Crash!

The smashup knocked Phil and the Reptar apart. Lil smiled like an angel as she toddled over to the crash site and picked up the desired toy. "See, Tommy?" she said sweetly.

Tommy nodded. He was impressed.

"Now you try it," Lil suggested.

Tommy crept up close to Dil. When the baby wasn't looking, Tommy captured the bear from his arms. Victorious, he turned to run away . . .

But a grubby little fist shot out and snatched it back.

"Tebby mine!" Dil squealed.

"Mine!" Tommy shouted back.

"Mine!"

"Give it!"

"Mine!"

Soon they were locked in a fierce tug-of-war.

Dil whacked Tommy with his rattle again and again.

But Tommy wouldn't let go.

"Gosh," Phil commented. "Tommy learns fast."

"Yeah," Lil agreed.

Whew! Tommy thought. *Boy, having a brother isn't easy!*

But deep down inside he couldn't help wondering: *Is this the way it's got to be?*

Angelica Pickles was so mad, she felt as if her two yellow pigtails would tie themselves in a knot.

Something very weird was going on here.

Her mom and dad always let her have her way. But not today!

She pouted royally as her dad parked their car in front of her cousin Tommy's house. She did *not* want to go in.

But her dad didn't even seem to notice. He just led her up the sidewalk to the front porch.

They stepped around Grandpa Lou, snoring in his rocker by the Reptar crate, and rang the bell.

Angelica waited patiently for someone to answer. But inside her head, she was pitching a fit.

Most of the time it was fun to come over to Cousin Tommy's house and pick on the babies. But not when her favorite TV show was on!

"But, Daddy," Angelica whined—whining often worked—"why can't I watch *Shirleylock Holmes* at our house? I'll never be able to hear it with that new baby squawkin' the whole time!"

"Now, sweetheart," Drew explained patiently. "Daddy's got to put in a little overtime today so

that Mommy won't be ashamed of his quarterly earnings."

Just then Stu opened the door, pulling his Reptar Wagon behind him.

Drew stepped back.

Whoa! Stu Pickles was a mess! His clothes were wrinkled, as if he'd slept in them. Except he looked as if he hadn't slept in days. Or shaved. Or—Drew wrinkled his nose—even taken a shower.

"Hi, Uncle Stu," Angelica chirped.

Stu opened his mouth to answer, when—

"WAAAAAHHHH!"

The sounds of Dil and Tommy's struggle sounded through the house.

"Excuse me," Stu said. "My tax deductions are crying."

"Yeah? Well, you can't deduct them if you don't have any income!" Drew reminded his brother.

But Stu wasn't even listening. Shaking his head, Drew headed back to his car and drove away.

Angelica stood on the doorstep and peered inside the house. Hmmm. All that crying sounded sort of interesting.

Well, well, Angelica thought as she went inside. *Maybe it isn't going to be such a wasted day after all.*

48

"Tommy! Dil!" she heard her Uncle Stu exclaim. "Boys. What are you doing?"

Tommy stopped shouting and smiled up at his dad. Everything would be all right now that his dad was here.

Tommy pointed at the teddy bear. *His* teddy bear.

Stu bent down and smiled at the baby. "Dil . . . what do you say we give Tommy a little turn with the bear, huh?"

He tried to remove the teddy bear from baby Dil's arms.

Dil screamed so loud, his father stumbled back and let go. "Or not," Stu said.

Dil smiled and wrapped his arms more tightly around the bear.

But now Tommy began to cry.

Stu was torn between his two children. How could he pick one over the other? Whatever he did, it would make one of his sons unhappy. *Man, this parenting business is tough. Especially when you haven't had any sleep!*

Tommy looked so sad. Stu decided there was only one thing to do. He lifted Tommy into his arms. "Hey, champ. Why don't you come with me for a minute? I've got something to show you that's even better than your old teddy bear."

Of course, Tommy couldn't understand most

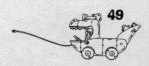

49

of his dad's words. But he liked the sound of his voice. And he liked being in his dad's arms even more.

Stu carried Tommy down into his basement workshop. He reached for something shiny that lay on the workbench. Then he showed it to Tommy.

It was an old gold pocket watch.

Tommy gazed at the shiny object in wonder.

"We weren't going to give you this until you were older," Stu told his son. "But I think now is the right time. Shiny, huh? And Grandpa Lou put your picture inside."

Stu pushed a tiny button to open the watch. Then he flipped open a secret lid underneath the big lid. Inside this second compartment was an engraving and a picture of Tommy and Dil.

Stu sat down on the bottom step with Tommy on his lap. "I know it's hard, Tommy. You have a little brother now." He chuckled softly. "Dil can be pretty tough to get along with, huh? But sometimes with little brothers . . . they aren't everything you hoped they'd be. That's why big brothers have got to have faith, and one day, you'll see. He'll change."

Tommy looked up curiously as his father wiped a tear from his eye. Then Tommy smiled as he cradled the watch in his hand.

"You've got responsibility now," Stu told him. "And I know I can trust that you'll stick by Dil's side and be a swell big brother."

Sniffling, Stu hugged his son.

"'Sponsitility," Tommy whispered as he curiously eyed the watch.

He wasn't sure what this shiny thing called 'sponsitility was. But he knew it was special.

He promised himself he would take good care of it—and Dil.

He was a big brother now.

He'd be the kind of brother that would make his dad proud.

Meanwhile, upstairs in the living room, Chuckie, Phil, and Lil had surrounded Mr. Pickles' strange new invention that he'd left in the middle of the floor.

"What is that, you guys?" Chuckie whispered.

"Reptar," Lil said in awe.

"On wheels," Phil added.

"Ooooooh!" the twins cooed, delighted.

"Oooooh!" Chuckie squealed, scared. "What do you think it's for?"

Phil shrugged. "I dunno."

Lil's eyes lit up. "I'll bet it could take us to the baby store."

"What?" Chuckie gasped.

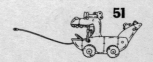

"Great idea, Lillian!" Phil replied. "We could take Dil to the hopsical and get Tommy's monies back!"

Lil and Phil dragged Dil out of his baby swing.

Dil hiccupped, but otherwise didn't seem to mind.

"Guys, guys!" Chuckie protested. "Tommy's not going to be happy about this."

"Well, he's sure not happy now," Lil pointed out to him.

"Yeah, he's tired and cranky all the time," Phil agreed.

"Well, uh, he's not the same ol' Tommy ever since Dil came," Chuckie admitted. "But—"

"You watch," Lil said with confidence. "Once Dil goes back to the baby store, Tommy will be happy again!"

Chuckie bit his fingernail. "Uh, I don't know about this . . ."

Phil and Lil plopped Dil into the seat of the Reptar Wagon. Lil stuffed his diaper bag in after him . . . just as Tommy toddled back into the room with his shiny new watch.

"What are you doing?" he asked his friends.

"We're taking Dil back to the hopsical, Tommy," Lil explained. "We're going to get your monies back!"

"What?" Tommy gasped. "You can't do that!

My mommy and daddy wanna keep him!"

"See, see!" Chuckie said. He *told* the twins it was a bad idea.

"Why?" Phil asked. "All he does is cry and poop."

"Oh, so do you," Tommy shot back.

"I don't cry that much," Phil protested.

"Well, *you* poop an awful lot," Tommy declared.

"Ah, look who's talking, Mr. Brown Pants!"

"I'm not a poopie monster!"

The arguing got louder and louder.

So loud that Angelica couldn't hear her program in the TV room.

"Stay tuned for *Shirleylock Holmes, Girl Detective,* right after these messages," the announcer said.

Finally! A commercial! Time to tell those babies to shut up! Angelica picked up her Cynthia doll and headed for the living room.

"We thought you'd be happy, Tommy!" Phil was saying.

"Well, I'm not!" Tommy replied. "Now take him out of the Reptar Wagon."

"I told you guys," Chuckie sang. "Toldyou-Itoldyou-Itoldyou . . ."

"Hey! Babies!" Angelica shouted, waving her arms around. "Knock it off! Cynthia and me are trying to watch TV!"

Angelica's words were just babble to Baby Dil. But he was dazzled by the Cynthia doll's turquoise eyes and spiky chopped-off hair as Angelica waved her about.

He had to have that doll! He grabbed her! "Mine. My dowwy."

"Hey!" Angelica snapped. "Hands off the merchandise, Pinky!"

She grabbed Cynthia by the feet. Dil hung on to her head. Another tug-of-war!

Suddenly Dil let go.

"Ahhhhhh!" Angelica flipped backward across the floor.

Phil and Lil looked at each other, impressed.

"Pretty good," they said together.

Tommy's brother was a fast learner, too.

Angelica got up and slowly turned around. How dare that baby! She stuck Cynthia in her pocket and stomped toward him. *Just wait till I get my hands on the little pest!*

But Tommy blocked her path. "Be nice, Angelica. He didn't mean it."

Angelica shoved Tommy aside. "You want to ride in a wagon?" she yelled at Dil. "I'll give you a ride . . . to outside space!"

With that, she gave the Reptar Wagon a good swift kick. *Cluuuuung!*

The wagon began to roll.

"Ow!" Angelica hopped up and down, clutching her foot. Now she was really mad! She tried to kick the wagon with her other foot and missed. Screaming, she fell flat on her bottom.

But then she heard the announcer on the TV in the next room. *Shirleylock Holmes, Girl Detective* was coming back on. "Oooh!" she cried, glaring at the babies. "My show!"

Angelica hobbled back into the TV room, still hollering and complaining. The babies could only stare.

They didn't notice as the Reptar Wagon, with Dil at the wheel, started to roll slowly toward the front door.

The open front door . . .

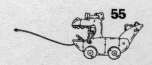

CHAPTER 6

"Weeeeee!" Baby Dil squealed.

Tommy and his friends whirled around just in time to see the Reptar Wagon roll out the front door and onto the front porch. It was picking up speed, fast.

"Dil!" Tommy cried.

"All aboard!" Lil whooped.

Tommy quickly jammed his gold watch into his diaper and dashed after the wagon. Phil and Lil ran after him to watch.

"Yippee!" Lil cried.

Chuckie watched in horror as his three friends

flopped into the moving wagon as it headed down the front steps.

He took one baby step backward. That looked way too scary. *No way am I gonna jump into a runaway Reptar Wagon,* he thought.

"Just walk away, Chuckie," he mumbled to himself. "Walk away . . ."

But there was one thing scarier than jumping into a runaway Reptar Wagon.

And that was being left behind.

"Wait for me!" Chuckie ran and dived into the Reptar Wagon as it clunked down the steps.

"Which way to the hopsical?" Phil shouted when they were halfway down the path.

"We're not going to the hopsical!" Tommy said when they bumped over the sidewalk.

"Well, we're going somewheres," Chuckie said as they shot through the grass beside the curb.

"This way!" Tommy cried.

"I can't look!" Chuckie squealed.

CLUNK! The wagon hopped the curb and rattled into the busy street.

Grandpa Lou, snoring on the front porch, slept through it all.

Moments later a delivery truck pulled into the Pickles' driveway. The driver hurried up the steps with his hand truck.

Grandpa Lou was dreaming about the old days,

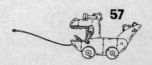

when he was in the army. "Please, Sarge," he mumbled in his sleep, "don't dig the latrine next to my tent."

"Uh, pardon me," said the busy driver. "Pick up for Pickles to Japan?"

"Take it away!" Grandpa Lou shouted, still dreaming about his sergeant. "Take it away!"

The driver shrugged and stuffed a receipt into Grandpa's hand. "Yeah, have a good day."

The driver taped the lid closed, then carted the crate to his truck.

Angelica was still glued to the tube watching *Shirleylock Holmes, Girl Detective.*

Out in the backyard Spike the dog howled.

"Shut up, Spike!" Angelica shouted. "Me and Cynthia are watching—"

Angelica froze.

She stuffed her hand into her pocket. But instead of her Cynthia doll, she pulled out—

A slobbery pacifier!

"Yech!" Angelica shrieked. "An old binky!"

Disgusting! She jumped up and stomped into the living room. "Nice try, babies. Now give me back my—"

She looked around. The babies were gone.

Her eyes flew to the open doorway.

One of Cynthia's tiny plastic doll shoes lay

on the ground. *Oh no!*

"CYNTHIA!" she screamed.

The babies had escaped—and kidnapped her favorite doll!

They weren't gonna get away with this!

Moments later Angelica, now in her roller skates, clumped across the Pickleses' backyard and untied Spike.

"They took Cynthia, Spike!" she told him. "C'-mon, you're going to be my bughound. We gotta search every doghouse, playhouse, treehouse, and dollhouse! I want those fugitives back in custerdy!"

Spike wasn't much of a bloodhound, but he did love to go for walks. He took off with a joyous bound, pulling a startled Angelica out the front door.

Moments after she left, Stu Pickles came up from the basement with an armload of tools and a cordless telephone cradled against his shoulder.

"Deed, just go to the spa and relax," he said into the phone. "Pop and I are doing fine taking care of the, uh—"

He stopped when he saw his father asleep on the porch. "Pop, where's the crate?"

"What? Huh?" Grandpa Lou snorted awake and looked around. When he saw the receipt in his hand, he shrugged. "Guess the delivery folks must have come."

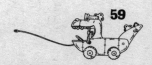

Stu was impressed by the service. The Reptar Wagon was gone, too, he noticed.

"Wow, they loaded 'er up and everything," Stu said in amazement.

A squawking from the phone reminded him that he still had Didi on the line. "Sure, honey," he said into the phone. "I'll let you talk to Tommy."

He looked around.

He didn't see Tommy.

He didn't see Dil, Phil and Lil, Chuckie, or Angelica.

Even worse—

He didn't hear them.

It had not been this quiet around the Pickleses' house for a whole year.

Stu covered the mouthpiece of the phone with his hand. "Uh, Pop," he said nervously, "where are the kids?"

Grandpa Lou scratched his head and looked around. "That's funny, they were here a minute ago, playing on the—"

Grandpa Lou gulped. The kids had been playing around the crate. The crate the delivery guy took away. He stared at the ground where the crate had been.

A half-empty baby bottle lay on its side dribbling milk onto the porch.

Where did Mommy's lap go?

My baby sister must be in here somewhere!

Hey, a baby store!

Tommy, meet your brother Dil.

Baby Dil, please share Mom and Dad with me!

Mine!

Oh no! Hold onto your diapies, babies!

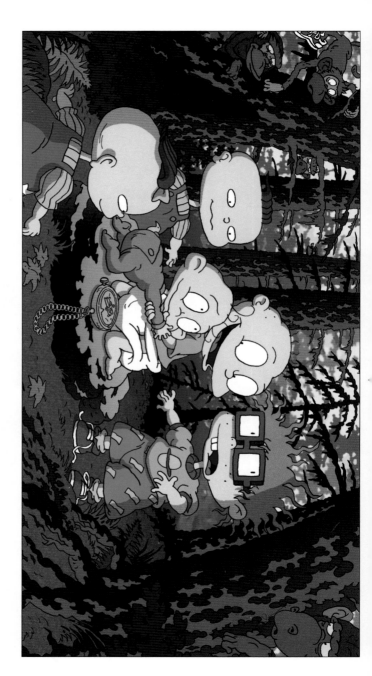

My 'sponsitility will get us through!

Stu and Lou looked at each other. They looked at the receipt in Lou's hand.

"The crate!" they screamed.

Stu stared at the phone in his hand. Oh, no. What was he going to tell Didi?

"Uh, honey?" Stu said, trying to sound normal, as if his kids and their friends hadn't just gotten shipped off to Japan in a packing crate! "I'm gonna have to call you back."

A short distance from the house, as the runaway Reptar Wagon zoomed down the hill, Dil snuggled into Chuckie's lap and did something new.

He got carsick. He threw up. All over Chuckie.

"Aw, Dil!" Chuckie groaned.

But all he could do was hang on as the Reptar Wagon streaked through a busy intersection.

Horns honked. Tires squealed. Cars swerved, just missing the little wagon full of babies.

The wind blew Cynthia's choppy hair as the babies whooshed through a playground. The Reptar Wagon caused a ten-tricycle pileup and kept right on going.

Next it zipped across the street, plowed through a mattress factory, and disappeared into the back of a delivery truck.

The good news was: The truck said JOE'S MATTRESS STORE. And it was full of mattresses. At least the babies had crashed into something soft.

The bad news was: The truck also said FREE DELIVERY WORLDWIDE.

Then the engine started up and the delivery truck pulled away.

ZOOM! Stu Pickles' hands gripped the steering wheel of his car as he roared past an AIRPORT EXIT sign.

"How could you fall asleep when you were supposed to be watching the kids?" he said to his dad.

Grandpa Lou didn't answer.

He was fast asleep.

Stu shook his head and kept driving. "We'll never find the babies with this jerk in front of us," he grumbled. "Road hog!" he shouted at the truck in front of him. He leaned on his horn to try and make the driver hurry up.

Stu read the company's name on the doors of the truck. JOE'S MATTRESS STORE.

No wonder, he thought. *This guy's probably always asleep on the job.*

Too bad he couldn't see inside the truck.

As it barreled over potholes in the road, five

babies inside giggled with glee as they bounced up and down on a big shipment of mattresses.

Stu thought the babies were in a crate being loaded onto a plane. He had to get to the airport before the plane took off for Japan!

But he'd never make it if he stayed behind this poky mattress truck. With a long blast of his horn, he whipped around the truck and into on-coming traffic. Brakes squealed and horns blared as Stu barely made it back into his lane before a head-on collision.

The truck driver, startled by Stu's driving, jerked his steering wheel and swerved to the right.

Then his eyes popped open wide. His truck was headed straight for a sign that said DEAD MAN'S CURVE!

Screaming, he leaped from the cab of the mov-ing truck.

Seconds later the truck full of mattresses—and five bouncing babies—crashed through a guardrail and plunged over the edge of the road.

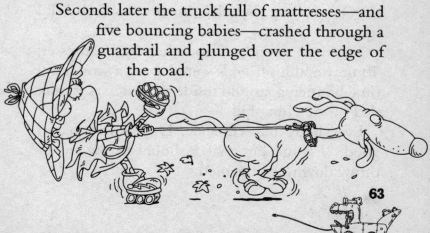

CHAPTER 7

"**T**his is more fun than picking noses!" Phil whooped.

"Or making bubbles in the bathtub," Lil squealed.

Safe and sound, surrounded by mattresses, Tommy and his friends were having a wonderful time bouncing around inside the truck as it hurtled down a long hill.

Everybody but Chuckie. He didn't look so good. "I don't know if I should throw up or throw down," he moaned.

As the truck plowed into the woods, a giant United Express cargo jet roared above it into the sky.

Inside the plane, several air crewmen had opened every crate on the plane—including Stu Pickles' crate to Japan.

"Sir," the pilot radioed to the tower, "I've turned this plane upside down, and there are no children."

Then he brought the controls around and turned the plane right side up again.

Down on the ground, Stu, Grandpa Lou, and several United Express workers huddled anxiously around a control panel inside the airport and listened to the pilot on the radio.

"I repeat," the pilot said, "negatory on the off-spring and the wagon."

Stu and Lou looked at each other.

Thank heavens the babies weren't on the plane!

But then—

If they weren't on the plane ... where were they?

At last the fun came to an end. The wild and crazy mattress ride crunched to a stop.

No one was hurt. The big, soft mattresses had kept them safe.

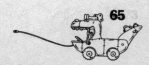

Tommy and the babies crawled out of the wrecked truck and looked around.

"Where are we?" Phil wondered, staring up at all the trees.

"I don't know," Tommy said. "It looks kind of like the park."

"Only biggerer!" Lil added.

"Biggerer?" Chuckie said. "This place is biggerer than the park and the backyard all put together! This is bad, you guys. This is bad."

Suddenly Dil let out a terrible little groan.

The babies jumped.

"Uh-oh, Tommy," Lil said. "I think your brother is broked again."

Tommy and his friends gathered around.

Dil did look awful. His face was scrunched up like a prune, and it was turning red.

"Oh, no!" Tommy had promised himself that he would take good care of his little brother. Look what a terrible job he'd done.

"Dil," Tommy asked worriedly, "are you okay?"

Dil didn't answer. His face just turned a deeper shade of red.

"I think he's going to explode!" Phil warned them, backing away.

Baby Dil whispered a single word.

"What?" Tommy asked.

Dil's eyes bulged as he repeated the word.
"POOPING!"

"EEEEWWWWWW!" The kids scattered in all directions.

But Tommy stood his ground. A baby's gotta do what a baby's gotta do, he always said.

"Well," Tommy said resolutely. "I guess we'll have to change his diapie."

"What do you mean, 'we'?" Phil said.

"Yeah," Lil replied. "He's your brother."

"Aw, c'mon, you guys," Tommy pleaded. "It can't be that bad."

They all looked down at Dil.

Yes, it could!

"What was that?" Stu said. He and Grandpa Lou had rushed back to the Pickles house to search for the missing children. "Dil?" he called hopefully, looking under the kitchen sink.

Not there.

"Pop," Stu moaned. "Where can they be? We've got to find them."

"Find what?" asked a curious voice from the doorway.

Stu jumped and conked his head on the drain.

Uh-oh. Didi's home! What in the world was he going to tell her?

Maybe he could stall her till he figured some-

thing out. Maybe he could tell her—

"Einstein here lost the kids," Grandpa Lou blurted out.

Didi froze.

Stu couldn't believe his father said that. "*I* lost the kids?" he exclaimed.

Grandpa shrugged. "See?"

Like a true Okeydokey Jones, Tommy steeled his nerves for the latest challenge: changing baby Dil's diaper.

Thanks goodness Lil had tossed his baby brother's diaper bag into the Reptar Wagon before they left home. So at least they had all the equipment. Now if they could just figure out how to use it!

I shoulda paid attention during all those diaper changes of my own, Tommy thought. Oh, well. He'd do the best he could.

The babies laid Dil out on a sort of flat tree stump. A giant cloud of baby powder swirled around them.

Everybody coughed.

"The powder goes on the baby, Tommy!" Lil reminded him.

"I'm doing the best I can," Tommy replied.

Tommy struggled with the diaper. Suddenly a gentle fountain squirted into the air.

"Look out!" Phil shouted.

Baby Dil just laughed, delighted with himself.

"Stop it, Dil!" Chuckie said.

"Aim him that way!" Phil said.

"Other way! Other way!" Chuckie said.

Tommy struggled to aim his brother away from his friends, who fled in several directions.

The stream of liquid squirted into the air, arcing above their heads. And hit a frog.

The frog jumped, and landed on Chuckie's face.

"Aaaaargh! Get it off!" Chuckie cried. "Get it off! Get it off!"

He stumbled into a tree and fell back, dazed. The frog hopped away.

Chuckie had never been more scared in his life. At least not since he could remember, which was back to yesterday. But as his heartbeat returned to normal, his fear turned to anger. He shouted at Tommy, "Your brother made a frog jump on me!"

"Dibbit!" Dil babbled, imitating the frog.

"Stop it," Chuckie snapped.

"Dibbit!" Dil repeated.

"You stop it!" Chuckie cried.

"Stobbit!"

"Dibbit!" Chuckie said.

Tommy stepped in to break up the fight.

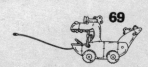

He knew they had a much bigger problem to worry about than messy diapers and dibbity frogs.

"Hey, guys," he said, "Maybe we should stop playing around and figure out how to get home from here."

Wherever "here" was.

The babies looked around.

They had no idea.

The babies looked at one another. Everyone was thinking the L word—*Lost.* But nobody wanted to say it out loud.

"But, Tommy," Lil said. "We don't even know where we are."

Good point, Tommy thought. That's when he remembered what his dad had given him before they left.

Tommy pulled the shiny pocket watch from the side of his diaper and held it up for all his friends to see. "That's okay. I've got my 'sponsitility!" he declared.

"What's a 'sponsitility?" Lil asked.

"Sounds yucky," Phil remarked.

Tommy shook his head. "It's what you get for bein' a big brother," he explained. "It's just like Okeydokey Jones uses when he has to find his way home."

Phil frowned. "I thought that was called a crumpus."

"Well, my dad gave it to me, and he called it a 'sponsitility,'" Tommy insisted.

"Where's it say to go?" Phil asked.

Tommy popped it open and studied the face of the watch.

The long hand and the short hand both pointed to the number twelve.

But Tommy couldn't read numbers yet. Or tell time. To him, the two hands of the pocket watch seemed to be pointing straight ahead—uphill.

"Straight up that hill," Tommy said with confidence. "C'mon, you guys. Forward, marge!"

A squad car squealed to a stop in front of the Pickles house. News of the missing babies had traveled fast. The street was already packed with cop cars, news vans, and the cars of worried relatives and friends.

Inside, the Pickles house was like command central. Policemen studied a neighborhood map on the wall. The phone rang nonstop. Neighbors made coffee. And seven very worried grown-ups tried to keep their hopes up. Stu and Didi Pickles. Drew and Charlotte Pickles. Betty and Howard de Ville. And Chuckie's dad, Chas.

Chas wrung his hands, worried sick about Chuckie.

Outside, Betty, handed out flyers with the kids' pictures.

At the center of the crowd, Lieutenant Klavin was interviewing Stu, hoping for some clues that might help them find the kids.

"I don't know, he's a baby," Stu said. "What's he weigh, Deed? Six, seven pounds?"

Didi still hadn't gotten over the shock. "I can't believe you left them with your father!" she kept saying. "The man slept through World War Two, for heaven's sake!"

Didi handed the Lieutenant a photo of Tommy.

The policeman looked at it curiously. "Uh, Mrs. Pickles, did your son have any enemies?"

Didi blinked. That was a funny question. "No."

"Uh-huh," the policeman mumbled as he scribbled a note on his pad. He looked very, very serious. "Any underworld, mob, or other criminal contacts?"

"He's a *baby!*" Didi exclaimed.

She snatched Tommy's picture back and stared at it with tears in her eyes. *Oh, Tommy, Dil. Where are you?* she cried to herself. *Will I ever see my babies again?*

The questions the police asked were not nearly as annoying as questions the reporters asked. Plus the reporters shoved microphones in Stu's and Didi's faces.

"Mr. Pickles," one shouted. "Is it true you shipped your own children to Tokyo in a wooden box?"

A reporter with an Australian accent asked, "Is it true a dingo ate your baby?"

And a third reporter asked, "Mr. Pickles, how many pecks of pickled peppers did you pick?"

Ch-Ch-Ch-Ch-Ch-

The media circus was suddenly interrupted by the roar of a helicopter. Slowly it landed on the lawn, air-blasting leaves, dresses, and toupees.

Rex Pester, a reporter known for sleazy news stories, climbed out. His cameraman followed like a well-trained dog as he walked to the front porch.

"Mr. Pickles!" Rex Pester said, shoving his microphone in Drew's face. "How does it feel knowing your brother lost your only daughter?"

"He *what?*" Drew said. Somehow, Rex Pester had gotten wind of Grandpa Lou's version of what happened.

"Share your pain," Rex Pester said.

Drew did—with his brother. "Yaaaaaaahhh!" he screamed as he jumped on Stu.

Flashbulbs went off like fireworks as the reporters rushed to photograph the drama of two brothers sharing their pain.

"You're breaking my arm!" Stu cried.

"Only 'cause I can't reach your neck!" Drew shouted as they tumbled to the ground.

Rex Pester calmly stepped over the fighting brothers to speak into the camera. "And there you have it. Two sour Pickles and . . ."

He plucked a picture of the babies out of a policeman's hand to show to the camera.

". . . young Tammy, baby Dale, the twins Bill and Jill, little Chunkie, and poor Amelia. All vanished without a trace. I'm Rex Pester, and I'll be back with more *Big Action News!*" Rex Pester never let little details like getting people's names right get in the way of a good story.

Suddenly Chas ran up with some real news. "Mr. Swenson on Sutter Street saw Angelica and Spike run through his garden, then head north on I-Ninety-nine!"

"My baby!" Charlotte cried.

Family, friends, reporters, and cops all jumped into their cars and sped off toward the highway.

Angelica was busy trying to control Spike, who was charging up the road, still dragging her along on her skates.

"Bad dog! Bad dog!" she shouted. *"Stop!"*

Spike obeyed. He stopped abruptly.

"AAAAAAAAHHHH!" Angelica went sailing past him, flung by the leash over the rail.

When she reached the end of the leash, she yanked Spike after her.

Screaming and howling, Angelica and Spike landed upside down in a bush.

Angelica growled.

Spike licked her face.

Deeper in the forest, the babies had the Reptar Wagon going up a hill.

To help keep their spirits up, they broke into a marching chant. Tommy sang the first verse, then the other babies answered.

"We are go-ing up the hill!" chanted Tommy.

"We'd go fast-er with-out Dil!" said Phil and Lil together.

"C'mon you guys he's not so bad!" Tommy answered.

"That froggie thing made me so mad!" yelled Chuckie.

"Nuh-huh!" Tommy sang.

"Uh-huh!" sang the others.

"Nuh-huh!"

"Uh-huh!"

"Some-times he is lots of fun!" Tommy said.

"He's a big pain in our buns!" said Phil and Lil.

"Chuckie, do you think so, too?"

Chuckie was limping from a stone bruise. "I just got a big boo-boo!" he whined.

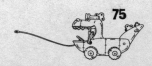

"Nuh–huh!"

"Uh–huh!"

"Nuh–huh!"

"Uh–huh!"

"He's just a baby don't you see?" Tommy sang.

"We'd like to leave him in a tree!" said Phil and Lil.

"He'll get bet–ter when he's growed!"

"We'd like to feed him to a toad!" said Phil and Lil.

"Doncha think he's kind of sweet?"

"All he does is poop and eat!" said Phil and Lil.

"Chuckie, don't you like him, too?"

"I got a rock inside my shoe," Chuckie replied.

Soon they had the Reptar Wagon almost to the top of the hill. Phil, Lil, and Chuckie were all together in front, pulling it by the handle. Tommy was alone in back, pushing. He was the only one who would get that close to Baby Dil, because he was playing bonkie with his rattle.

Bonkie was played by hitting with the rattle. Tommy's fingers were getting the worst of it. But Tommy just tried to ignore it and keep everyone's spirits up.

"Good job, you guys!" Tommy cheered. "Ow—" Another bonk from Dil.

"We're almost there! Ow!—" Another bonk.

"Good Dil. Ow! Play nice! Ow!" More bonks.

Phil was feeling okay. "Not much fun back there, is it," he called to Tommy.

"Oh, we're doin' okay," Tommy called back. He gave Dil his best smile. "That's some good hitting, there, Dilly!"

"I'm tired, Tommy," Chuckie complained.

"Keep goin', Chuckie!" Tommy said. "We're gonna see our houses any minute!"

Tommy leaned closer to Dil. "'Fact, the growed-ups are prolly on the other side right now. And we'll all go have a nice nappie and some hot choclie and pudding and—"

Dil bonked Tommy one more time with his rattle.

"Stop it, Dil!" Tommy shouted.

Finally they reached the top. Tommy didn't even realize it—until he heard the others gasp.

"Oh, no!" Chuckie croaked.

Tommy peeked around from the back of the Reptar Wagon to see what was wrong.

Below them, as far as they could see, stretched a vast forest.

"We can't see our houses from here, Tommy," Lil complained.

"We can't see any houses from here," Phil added.

They frowned at Tommy as if it were his fault.

"We're doomed," Chuckie moaned. "Doomed, doomed, doomed!"

Not too far away, by the side of a lonely road, Lieutenant Klavin was showing something to Mr. and Mrs. Pickles. "Mrs. Pickles," the policeman said firmly, "I know this is hard for you, but could you identify this binky?"

He showed her a dirt-caked pacifier. Dil's.

Mrs. Pickles nodded sadly and hugged Stu.

Climbing the big hill had made the babies tired. And crabby. Especially Phil, who was crabby anyway. "It's all Dil's fault! Right, Chuckie?" he said.

Chuckie glanced at his best friend, Tommy. He sort of thought what Phil said was true. But he didn't want to make his best friend mad. So he tried to stay neutral. All he could think to say was, "Uh . . ."

Tommy got mad. He backed against the wagon, standing up for Dil. "Nuh-unh! This never woulda happened if you hadn't a putted him in the wagon in the first place! Right, Chuckie?"

"Uh . . . nuh-huh-uh-nuh!" Chuckie said. It was getting harder and harder to stay out of the fight.

Lil chimed in on Phil's side, of course. "It's not our fault you gots a bad, naughty, stinky baby for a brother."

"He's not naughty," Tommy insisted. "He's just—"

Right in the middle of the argument, Tommy noticed a draft.

He glanced down. Somehow Dil had pulled Tommy's diaper tapes loose. Tommy stood as still as a statue as the white, crinkly material slowly glided over his knees and plopped down around his ankles.

"A baby," Tommy finished, staring at his diaper in horror. "How can you be mad just because you're um, uh . . . standing there all nakey. No! I mean, I'm sure he's just trying to help. And 'sides, we're all just hot, 'splorin' all day in the woods. . . ."

How could he think straight with his diaper in the dirt?

Dil hiccupped happily.

That just made Phil more angry. "Those hip-ups are really startin' to bug me," he griped.

"Face it, Tommy," Lil said. "Havin' a baby brother just isn't what you espected."

Tommy frowned. He couldn't really blame his friends for saying all those mean things about Dil. He could be kind of annoying. Tommy pulled up his diaper.

But every time Tommy looked at his 'sponsitility, his father's words came back to him. *I know I can trust that you'll stick by Dil's side and be a swell big brother. . . ."* Tommy had no idea what the

words meant, but the way his dad had said them sounded important.

Tommy held his 'sponsitility in his hand. He opened the case. The hands pointed straight and true under a clear, colorless glass cover. There was not a scratch on it. He was going to keep it that way, too. And he was going to live up to his 'sponsitility, always.

"Hey you guys!" Chuckie gasped. "Look!"

Tommy looked into the forest where the hands on his 'sponsitility were pointing.

Smoke! Rising from a chimney! Just over the hill—a cabin—and someone was there!

"Somebody's house!" Chuckie said.

Tommy looked at the pocket watch, totally amazed. "Wow. My 'sponsitility *does* work!" It was like magic.

Phil didn't want to believe it. "Who'd have a house way out here in the forest?" he wanted to know.

"Maybe it's a princess, or a fairy," Lil guessed.

"Or a witch that's gonna put us in the oven and cook us up," Chuckie suggested.

Tommy's eyes lit up. "Maybe a lizard lives there!" he hoped.

Chuckie scrunched up his face. "A lizard?"

"You know," Tommy said. "A big guy with a pointy hat that grants wishes! Alls we gots to do is knock on the door and say we wanna go home, see, then everything will be back to Norman."

Excited now, Tommy began to toddle. "C'mon, guys. We're off to see the lizard!"

Two steps later he tripped and fell. The others rushed to his side.

"Tommy, are you okay?" Chuckie asked.

"I'm fine," Tommy said. "Uh, just tripped in a . . . little hole, that's all."

But it wasn't an ordinary hole. This hole was shaped like a paw print. A huge paw print. And there was another hole just like it, right beside the one Tommy was sitting in.

"Gosh," Chuckie observed. "It looks kinda like Spike's feet, only if he was giant."

"I saw feetprints like that in our storybook," Phil told them. "A woof made 'em and then he ate that little red riding girl."

Chuckie gasped. "A woof ate a girl?"

Phil shrugged. "They got her out."

"I don't think it's a woof, Chuckie," Tommy said quickly. "If it was, we'd hear him say . . ." Tommy threw his head back and opened his mouth wide.

"OWOOOOO!"

Birds squawked and scattered into the sky. Squirrels scampered up the trunks of trees.

Tommy closed his mouth, looking confused.

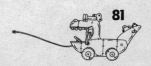

"That was pretty good," Phil said.

In a small voice Tommy said the words that no one wanted to hear: "I didn't do anything."

Then who did?

For about three seconds no one spoke.

Then they all screamed at once.

"AAAAHHHHHH!"

The babies piled into the Reptar Wagon, and it began to roll down the hill. As it gained speed, the Reptar roared, "I AM REPTAR! I'M THE PERFECT CHILDREN'S TOY!"

"Did you see the woof?" Tommy shouted into the wind.

Chuckie huddled close to Tommy. "I don't know what he looks like!"

"Teeth!" Phil explained. "Teeth and fur! And teeth!"

Suddenly Dil yanked hard on the steering wheel and aimed them at a tree.

Tommy gasped and struggled to get the wheel away from his brother. "No, Dil. No!"

"Mine!" Dil insisted.

But Tommy wrenched the wheel around just in time to miss the tree and pick up another, steeper downhill trail.

On a deeply rutted dirt fire road a short distance away in the middle of nowhere, two forest rangers bounced around in the cab of an official government truck.

The beefy one behind the wheel was named Frank. Beside him was a worried-looking woman dressed in an identical park ranger's uniform. Only hers was neatly pressed. Her name was Margaret.

She was new on the job.

"I just knew that someday I'd end up getting into one of these National Parks, which you know are a lot bigger than the ones in the city, although I have to say you people don't really have a lot of grass out here. And where are the drinking fountains?"

Frank kept a steady eye on the road. "Yes, well, out here in the country you have to be just a little tougher." He reminded himself that Margaret was going through a period of adjustment. It must be tough switching from a city park to a park in the wilderness. He tried to be patient.

"Margaret?" he said. "I'm sure you've run afoul of many a scary pedestrian. But out here we have what you might call . . . hmm, how shall I put it?"

He wanted to make it as terrifyingly real for her as possible.

"Actual danger!" he said at last.

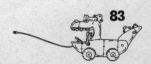

"Danger?" Margaret asked.

"Grizzlies that'll rip the top off your car! Bob-cats! Wolves! Wolverines—which are something entirely different!"

Margaret glanced around nervously.

And that's when she saw it.

A quick glimpse of the Reptar Wagon as it burst through the woods, flashed across the road behind them, and vanished into the undergrowth on the other side.

"And dragons?" Margaret asked Frank.

Frank frowned. "What?"

"Dragons!" Margaret squealed. "You have dragons out here? Nobody told me that! Oh, my gosh—this is like my total destiny!"

Meanwhile, on the Reptar Wagon, Chuckie had spotted Margaret, too. "Tommy!" he cried. "I sawed some growed-ups! Stop!"

"I don't know how!" Tommy yelled. He yanked a knob and pushed buttons on the Reptar's control panel.

Nothing seemed to be hooked up.

"Well, I hope you figger it out," Lil complained, pointing ahead, "'cause I didn't bring no bathey suit."

Tommy looked where she pointed.

Up ahead the trail they were on crossed the

rapids—the fastest flowing part of the wild river.

"Aaaaaaaahhhhhhhhhh!!!" they all screamed. Then, at the last minute, Tommy pulled a red knob that made everyone crash together at the front of the wagon.

The Reptar stopped right at the very edge of the riverbank. The wagon's front wheels spun free over the rushing water.

"Quick, guys," Tommy shouted. "Let's call the growed-ups!"

"Help! Help!" they cried.

They were so busy calling for help that no one noticed as Dil reached for the red knob on the brake handle. He turned it, fascinated.

Then Tommy noticed. "Dil! No!" he shouted. But it was too late.

The brake handle slipped out of Dil's hand and slammed against the control panel. The Reptar Wagon plunged into the current and took a soaking in the very first wave.

But the Reptar Wagon was designed for just such an emergency! "Aqua Reptar, ENGAGE!" it roared.

The babies stared, amazed, as the wagon's tail began to turn like a propeller and lower itself into the water. Inflatable pontoons expanded along the sides.

The Reptar Wagon was ready for whitewater!

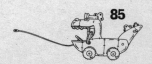

CHAPTER 8

Back at the park rangers' office, Margaret was flipping through the TV channels. "I'm telling you, I saw something out there," she insisted. "There's gotta be something on TV about it. Imagine, we spotted an actual North American dragon."

Ranger Frank rolled his eyes. "I think I'll let you take all the credit on this one," he said.

"No, no, no!" Margaret insisted. "You keep an

eye out for it while I find the news." She clicked
past game shows, the shopping channel, cartoons,
and a talk show.

She stopped when she saw Rex Pester in a live
news bulletin. Maybe this was it!

". . . And as this heartrending search for the
children continues, all of us have to ask ourselves
the hard questions," Rex Pester said sternly.

Frank shook his head. "You'd think if people
are gonna actually *have* children, they could at
least *try* to keep an eye on them."

Just then something in the stream below the
cabin caught his eye. *No. It can't be . . .*

"AHHH! The dragon!" he yelled. "I just saw it!
I saw it!"

"Where? Where?" Margaret cried. She was trying to figure out how to use Frank's huge binoc-
ulars. "Do I look through here? Where? Here?"

On a narrow stretch of road that curved around a
steep hillside, Grandpa Lou adjusted the straps of
his World War II search-and-rescue gear. Then he
bent over for a closer look at the ground.

"Bingo!" he yelled. "Lookie here!"

The other adults rushed over to him.

"A wrapper from a Cynthia Sweet Bar!"
Grandpa Lou announced. Everyone marveled at
the discovery.

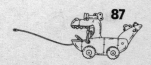

"My angel!" Drew cried. "She's been here!"

Grandpa Lou nodded wisely. "Yep. I figger she's trackin' the sprouts." Then his chest puffed up a little. "It's the Pickles blood. I myself spent fifteen days tracking Sitting Bull through the Northwest Territory. The year was eighteen—"

But before he could go on—and on, and on!— Howard and Chas climbed out of a ravine, tooting on their whistles.

"Over here!" Howard called to them.

Chas let his whistle drop on the cord that held it around his neck. "We found some wheel tracks and baby footprints heading into the woods!"

Stu gasped. "They must be in my Reptar Wagon!"

"It's the perfect children's toy," Drew said sarcastically. "You and your stupid inventions!"

A light went on in Stu's brain. He snapped his fingers. "My stupid inventions! That's it!"

Betty snatched a policeman's bullhorn and switched it on full blast. "All right, the pups are in the woods!" she barked. "You men, follow those tracks! We'll head to the ranger station and start a search from there! Now move out!" The policemen responded immediately to the bullhorn. Stu, Chas, and Grandpa Lou piled into Stu's car.

"Stu!" Didi called. "Where are you going?"

"Trust me," Stu hollered out the window to his wife. "I have a plan."

As the rescue units headed into the hills, Rex Pester gave his cameraman a nod and made a concerned face.

"And so the tender babes have strayed into the woods," Pester began. "Will they get eaten by a bear? Will they freeze in the night? Or will they run out of clean diapers?"

A thought crossed the newsman's mind, and he leaned closer to the camera. "Perhaps they'll run out of clean diapers, freeze, and then get eaten by a bear!"

Rex Pester's eyes gleamed in delight. This was one big news story!

WHACK! Betty canned his head with the bullhorn. As Pester struggled to remove it, he signed off, "I'm Rex Pester for *Big Action News!*"

At a wide bend in the stream, calm water sparkled under shafts of golden sunlight slanting through a canopy of trees. Ducks and otters frolicked among the cattails along the bank. A baby duck paddled happily into the lazy current and swam right into the shadow of—a massive aquatic beast!

"Quack-quack-quack-quack-quack!" the baby duck honked in terror as it looked up into the terrifying face of—

Reptar!

Otters ducked below the cattails. Ducks air-walked across the top of the water in emergency takeoff formation. Snakes slithered for the banks. Even the fish fled.

The Reptar Wagon—now turned pirate ship—sailed merrily down the stream.

"Slob the poop deck, Mr. Phil!" Tommy barked, delighted to discover that fate had made him captain of his own ship. He turned to Chuckie, his right-hand baby. "Hoist the ankle, Number One!"

"My eye, Captain!" Mr. Phil shouted with glee.

Chuckie tried to figure out what an ankle was. And how did you hoist it?

"Mr. Chuckie! Honk the horn some more!" Captain Tommy ordered. He pointed at some ducks swimming a few yards downstream. "There are still chickies in our way!"

Mr. Chuckie was delighted to receive an order that he could understand. With great zeal, he pushed the horn again, which made the Reptar Wagon roar, "I AM REPTAR! I WILL DESTROY YOU!"

Captain Tommy gazed down the bend of river

as far as he could see. He was ready to sail round the world!

"Guys," Chuckie said mournfully, "I'm hungry." He sighed.

He couldn't help but think about what it would be like if he were home right now, instead of sailing down a stream in a talking dinosaur pirate ship.

Chuckie's eyes glazed over as he lost himself in the vision. "Right about now my dad would be making me a fried baloney sandwich," he gushed. "Ummm . . . I can almost smell it burning. Ooh! It tastes all crunchy and—"

"Stop it, Chuckie!" Captain Tommy ordered his Number One. "You're making me hungry."

Lil glanced nervously at her twin brother. Her growling stomach was making her crabby, and now she turned on him. "Phillip's got worms!" she revealed.

"Oh, really?" Chuckie said, his face lighting up.

"No!" Phil insisted.

"Yes, you do, Phillip!" Lil argued. She grabbed his diaper, dug in, and yanked out a clear plastic package. It was stuffed with long colorful strips of soft, chewy candy.

"Dummy Worms!" Tommy and Chuckie cried out.

"Uh, hey," Phil chuckled nervously. "Where'd they come from?"

But before Captain Tommy could decide what to do, Dil snatched the bag out of Lil's hand. "Mine! Mine! Mine! Mine! Mine!" he hollered. He shook the plastic bag like a baby rattle.

Not good. The package split like a *piñata*. Dummy Worms scattered all over the deck of the ship. With a shriek, the babies scrambled to grab their share.

Chuckie spotted several worms sinking slowly in the water beside the boat. He stuck his hand in just as a huge trout darted toward the candy bait.

CHOMP! The fish clamped its tiny but sharp teeth into Chuckie's hand.

"SHAAARK!" he screamed, yanking everything—his hand, the Dummy Worm, and the trout—out of the water.

"Hey!" Lil giggled. "Chuckie caughts a fishie!"

Chuckie hopped around in the boat, trying to shake the fish off. The wagon tipped dangerously.

All the rocking made it even harder for Tommy, who was trying to pull the Worm bag out of Baby Dil's amazing grasp.

"Chuckie, stop playing around!" Tommy complained.

Suddenly Chuckie was in trouble. He teetered

over the side rail of the Reptar Wagon. "Help me, Tommy!" he screamed. "AAAAHH!"

But just then Baby Dil wriggled out of Tommy's grasp and skated across the wagon.

"Dil!" Tommy cried.

But Chuckie needed help, too!

Tommy looked both ways. What should he do?

But there was no time to think.

Tommy grabbed Dil . . .

Just as Chuckie screamed and disappeared over the side.

"Man overboat!" Lil shouted.

Tommy clutched Dil in his arms. He felt wonderful . . . and horrible. He'd saved his baby brother. But he let his best friend fall out of the boat!

He peered over the railing. *Now what?* Should he dive in to save him?

Gulp. Tommy didn't even know how to swim in the bathtub, much less in a stream!

But suddenly something amazing happened.

A flotation ring on a rope ejected from the back of the wagon. It made a perfect ringer around Chuckie. Then the Reptar Wagon automatically reeled Chuckie in with such speed that his rear end made a wide wake in the water, just like a water-skier.

After cutting a few zigzags, Chuckie swung wide as the boat turned. He skied up a fallen tree

93

in the water. And did a giant slalom—splat!—right into the boat.

Baby Dil laughed so much, he gave himself the hiccups.

But Chuckie didn't laugh or clap, even though he'd been rescued. Instead, he looked hurt and disappointed.

"Tommy," he asked tearfully, "why didn't you help me?"

Tommy's heart twisted beneath his baby blue T-shirt. How could he explain? "I'm sorry, Chuckie," he began. "But Dil—he needed me and he's . . . just a . . ."

"Just a baby," his friends said together.

"Yeah, well, I ain't ezactly a growed-up myself!" Chuckie shot back. "That big shark was tryin' to eat me, and you didn't even care."

But Tommy *did* care! He started to explain.

Suddenly a strange roar drowned out his words.

The babies turned and stared downstream.

A waterfall!

"ARRRGHHHH!"

The babies grabbed on to the Reptar pirate ship as they hurtled over the falls.

CHAPTER 9

Splash!

The babies got soaked. But lucky for them, the waterfall was small. And the Reptar's floats kept them upright.

Only now the woods seemed even deeper and darker.

Tommy swallowed, then said cheerfully, "That wasn't so bad."

Phil tapped him on the shoulder and pointed downstream. A cloud of fine mist filled the width

of the river all the way to the treetops. A deep pounding sound told them it was another water-fall.

Only this time, it was a big one.

As the Reptar Wagon picked up speed in the current, Chuckie made a last request.

"Guys, next time just let the fish eat me."

But Tommy wasn't ready to give up. "Hard to porkside!" he shouted. "Turn! Turn around!" He wrestled with the wheel, but the current was too strong. "Help me, you guys!"

His friends jumped to help with the wheel. But just as the wagon started to turn, Baby Dil grabbed the wrong side and pulled in the opposite direction.

"Dil, no!" Tommy shouted.

He grabbed his brother around the waist and dragged him off the wheel. His friends yanked the wheel and turned.

At the last possible moment they managed to turn the Reptar Wagon. It charged ashore, just beneath an old railway bridge, where it hit a log and flipped the babies into the undergrowth.

"Whoooooooaaaaaa!" they yelled.

Tommy landed hard and the watch was knocked out of his diaper. *My 'sponsitility!* He scrambled after it and caught it just in time to keep from losing it in the water.

He carefully dried it off on his T-shirt, then joined the others near the railway trestle.

Clouds began to gather overhead.

"Do ya think we'll still be able to find the Lizard's house, Tommy?" Chuckie asked.

"Uh, sure, Chuckie!" Tommy said cheerfully. "Long as I got my 'sponsitility, we'll never be losted!"

"So," Phil asked, looking around, "which way are we supposed to go?"

Tommy studied his watch.

Uh-oh. That was weird. This time the hands were pointing in two different directions. *What did that mean?* Tommy didn't have a clue. "Um, uh . . ." Tommy began. What would Okeydokey Jones do? *Would he sit around being confused?*

No way!

Tommy made a choice. He picked a path. Then he pointed like a brave explorer and shouted, "That way!"

Tommy led them around a tree, concentrating on his watch as if it were a compass. His loyal friends followed.

Around the tree they went.

"Hey, lookie!" Chuckie called out. "Footprints!" He held his foot out next to one of the prints. It was almost exactly the same size. That could only mean one thing.

"There's other babies around here!" he cried.

Lil stuck her own foot into one of the footprints. It fit perfectly—like Cinderella and the glass slipper. "Wait a minute," she said. "Those are *our* feetprints, Chuckie!"

"You're leading us around in a circle, Tommy!" Phil complained.

Tommy stared at his watch. He didn't understand. "It was working before . . ."

"I don't think it ever worked," Lil snapped. "I think your 'sponsitility's broked—just like your brother!"

"My brother is not broked!" Tommy shouted.

"He tried to send us into the big ja-suzy," Phil accused, pointing back at the waterfall they'd just missed.

"We could have been drownded!" Lil agreed.

"He didn't mean it, you guys!" Tommy explained. "He was just playin'!"

"Well, I'm tired of playin' with him," Phil declared.

"Me, too!" Lil said.

Tommy couldn't believe it. Why were the twins ganging up on a little baby? But before he could say anything more, Chuckie pulled on his shirttail.

"Hey, guys . . ." Chuckie gasped. "Clow . . . clow . . ."

"What is it, Chuckie?" Lil asked. He looked like he'd seen a ghost.

Chuckie pointed into the woods.

A huge white face with bloodred lips and blazing blue eyes stared at the babies through the trees.

"CLOOOOOWWWWWWWNNNNNN!" Chuckie screamed. He scrambled behind Tommy, trembling in terror.

But Tommy noticed there was something funny about the clown face. It wasn't moving!

He led the other babies through the bushes into a gravel clearing beneath the railroad trestle to investigate.

The clown face was painted on the side of a wrecked train car. Part of a circus train that had jumped the tracks. It wasn't really watching them.

But they still had a funny feeling . . .

Phil, Lil, and Chuckie ran ahead to explore the train wreck, leaving Tommy to pull the Reptar Wagon all by himself.

"Wow," Phil said, admiring the train car. "You never know what you're gonna find in the forest, do you?"

Suddenly the sound of circus music filled the air around them.

Tommy wondered later if they'd been dreaming.

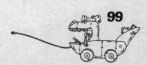

If they were, it was a dream they were all having to-gether.

A little monkey cranked an old music box. An-other monkey dropped from a tree. Then anoth-er. And another.

Soon they were surrounded by monkeys. In the circus act the monkeys performed a song and dance show! The monkeys sang and Phil, Lil, and Chuckie were swept up into the monkey's wild dance. Tommy started to join in, too.

But he stopped when Dil began to cry.

"What?" Tommy complained. "What do you want?"

"Hungy," Baby Dil said. "Hungy."

Tommy suddenly looked very tired. He'd been a good big brother all day. He'd even chosen Dil over his best friend. Would he always have to put his baby brother first? Couldn't he do what he wanted to do sometimes? "But I really wanna go play with the monkeys!"

"Hungy!" Baby Dil insisted.

Tommy sighed and dug around in Dil's diaper bag. At last he found one tiny jar of baby food. He tried to feed it to his brother, but only about half went in Dil's mouth. The rest of it dribbled on their clothes and the diaper bag.

One of the monkeys came up and sniffed. Yummy! Bananas! The monkey grabbed the diaper bag and started dragging it away.

"Hey, come back here, you monkey!" Tommy scolded.

Meanwhile, the monkeys had been swinging Chuckie around in the trees. He was right above Tommy when he fell out.

"Help!" Chuckie yelled, landing on top of Tommy.

Tommy pushed him off. "Quit playing around, Chuckie. Watch my brother, I gotta go get the diapie bag!"

Chuckie's lip trembled as he held his hurt elbow. But it was his feelings that mostly hurt. "But, Tommy—"

But Tommy was gone, toddling full speed after the diaper bag.

Chuckie stared after his best friend and felt a tear in his eye. Things just weren't the same between him and Tommy anymore. Not with that baby around.

He glared at Dil, who was still sitting in the Reptar Wagon.

Another little monkey was sniffing him, drawn to the smell of bananas. Then the monkey tried to pull Dil out of the wagon!

"Hey!" Chuckie shouted. "Leave him alone! He's not a 'nanner!" He ran over to the Reptar Wagon and pulled Dil out. Then he shooed the

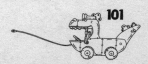

monkey away.

The monkey didn't like that.

He chattered for reinforcements.

More monkeys arrived right away.

Tug-of-war! Only this time it wasn't a toy in the middle. It was Dil!

"No, hey!" Chuckie cried, pulling on Dil. "Hey, guys, help!" he shouted to his friends. "This monkey is trying to take Tommy's brother!"

Phil wasn't sure that was such a bad idea. "So?"

"Just help me, okay?" Chuckie snapped.

With a shrug, Phil and Lil came to help on Chuckie's side. But before long the monkeys had them outnumbered.

"Hey! Don't touch my hair!" Chuckie yelled at a monkey that was using Chuckie's red hair for a handhold while it went for his glasses.

Dil laughed and joined the fun by pulling on Phil's hair.

"What do we do?" Lil squealed. They were losing the tug-of-war.

"Let go! Let go!" Chuckie yelled at the monkey. It had his glasses now.

But Phil and Lil thought he was telling them

to let go of Dil. "Okay." And they did.

Instantly some of the monkeys dragged Dil away through the woods.

Chuckie's monkey was through with his glasses now. It tossed them aside and scampered off with the other baby-snatcher monkeys.

"Oh, this is just great!" Chuckie moaned, walking around blind. "I tell ya it can't get any worser than—"

CRUNCH!

Chuckie felt something break beneath his shoe.

It sounded like . . . *oh, no.* His glasses! He picked them up and put them on.

"—worser than this."

The view through Chuckie's glasses was cracked, kind of like a kaleidoscope. It looked as if Phil and Lil had suddenly become quintuplets.

"Well, at least the monkeys are gone," Phil pointed out.

"Yeah," Lil added brightly. "And tooked Baby Dil with them!"

Chuckie sat down and buried his face in his hands.

Tommy already didn't seem to like him much anymore. What was he gonna do when he found out that Chuckie let the monkeys run off with his baby brother?

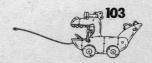

CHAPTER 10

On the crest of a hill where it seemed as if the whole forest lay before her, Angelica Pickles sat down on a lumpy log.

She was tired. And sweaty. And worried about her doll.

"Oh, Cynthia," she wailed. "Are they taking care of you? Will they know to comb your hair, or change you into your sports jumper with matching neckerchief at lunchtime?"

She doubted it. Not those dumb babies. They didn't know anything about fashion dolls.

"Ooh, when I get my hands on those babies, they're gonna be wearin' their dirty diapers on their heads!" she vowed.

But something was wrong with one of her

skates. When she stood up, the wheel shot out from under her.

She landed hard on her rear. "Hey!" she griped. "My rolly-blade is cracked!" Angrily she yanked off the skate.

Unknown to her, a creature crept toward her through the forest.

A gray wolf!

Its paws were perfectly silent. Its yellow eyes were perfectly fixed on her. Soon its gaping jaws were perfectly positioned to gobble up one little girl in one quick bite!

"Ugh! Pee-yoo!" Angelica complained, pinching her upturned nose. "I smell dog breath!" She tossed the no-good broken roller skate over her shoulder.

Conk! It smashed the big gray wolf smack in the nose.

With a whimper, the beast turned and bolted into the forest.

Angelica got up and headed over the crest of the hill with renewed energy. She'd save poor Cynthia from those babies if it was the last thing she ever did!

Not too far away, Chuckie and the twins huddled around the Reptar Wagon.

They were all talking at once.

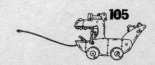

"Shhh!" Phil said. "Here comes Tommy!"

"Put the blankey on him!" Lil whispered.

Quickly they tucked Dil's blanket into the wagon, covering up the little guy inside.

Tommy staggered over to his friends, dragging the diaper bag behind him. It was dirty and torn, but still in one piece. "I gotta finish feeding my brother," he said.

Chuckie looked helplessly at Phil.

Phil looked at Lil.

"Uh . . . I don't think he's hungry, Tommy," Lil said.

"Yeah," Chuckie added. "And, uh, besides, he's . . ."

Tommy leaned over the wagon and pulled back the blanket.

"A monkey!" Tommy squealed.

A diapered baby monkey lay on Dil's pillow, sucking on a bottle.

Phil pretended to be totally surprised. "Well, look at that!"

Tommy's jaw dropped open. "My brother turned into a monkey?" he shrieked.

But before anyone could begin to make up an explanation—

Kablam! A crack of thunder startled them.

Chuckie grabbed Tommy's arm. "Come on, Tommy, we gotta get outta here."

Tommy pulled away. "I can't go home with my brother being a monkey!"

"Oh, but, Tommy," Chuckie begged, glancing up at the scary black clouds, "we gotta get to the lizard's house."

Tommy's eyes lit up. "That's it! I'll get the lizard to wish him back into a people." He grabbed the Reptar Wagon and started pulling.

His friends looked at one another.

"But the lizard's only gonna give us one wish!" Phil argued.

"Yeah," Chuckie said. "And if you use it up on Dil, how are we gonna get home?"

"He's my *brother,* Chuckie," Tommy explained. "I hafta wish him back!"

"You can't do that!" Lil insisted.

"Yes, I can!" Tommy argued back. "What would you do if Phil turned into a monkey?"

"That's different," Lil said. "I like Phillip. 'Sides, you'd be wastin' your wish anyway, 'cause that's not even your brother—"

Oops!

Phil and Chuckie shot Lil a dirty look.

Tommy looked confused.

Chuckie started blabbering. "Uh, what Lillian means is, um, the monkeys kind of took Baby Dil, and we just . . ." He winced. "We thought you wouldn't mind a baby monkey instead."

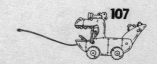

107

"What?" Tommy exclaimed.

Lil tried to reason with him. "Look, Tommy. Nobody likes your brother."

"Yeah," Phil put in. "Since he came, we never have no fun anymore."

Tommy glared at his friends. "We have fun all the time."

"Oh, like what?" Lil shot back. "This dumb aventure where your Dil gots us losted in the forest?"

Phil's mind was made up. "We're going to find that lizard, Tommy," he declared. "You can find your brother by yourself."

Tommy didn't know what to say. How could Phil and Lil turn against him like this? Oh, well. He couldn't worry about that now. He and Chuckie would just have to find Dil all by themselves. "C'mon, Chuckie, I need your help."

Chuckie didn't come on.

He shoved his broken glasses up on his nose and peered nervously at the sky. It would be dark soon. Awful dark.

"Sorry, Tommy," Chuckie said softly.

Tommy couldn't believe it. Not Chuckie, too! "But you're my bestest friend!"

"Oh, yeah?" Chuckie shot back. "Well, if I'm your bestest friend, then how come when I got throwed up on, you didn't help me? Huh? *Huh?*

And when I fell overboard, you didn't help me. And then when the fish was eating my hand, where was you, huh? And when the monkey dropped me, you didn't even care about my boo-boo . . ." Chuckie rubbed his elbow to emphasize his point.

"All you cared about was dumb old Baby Dil," Chuckie said sadly. "You don't even play with me no more."

Tommy felt sick—kind of like he had an upset tummy. Only the feeling was higher up, nearer his heart.

Lil gave Tommy a hard look. "Face it, Tommy. You don't gots a bestest friend no more. All you gots is a brother."

Tommy wanted to say he was sorry. He didn't mean to hurt anybody's feelings. Especially Chuckie's.

But his friends all seemed to be ganging up on him.

And his baby brother was still lost.

A big brother's got to do what a big brother's got to do.

"Well, fine," Tommy said at last. "I'll go find him by myself."

Phil and Lil stomped off. Chuckie hung his head and wandered off into the trees.

Tommy sadly watched him go.

He'd made his choice, but that didn't mean he

liked it. He definitely didn't like it.

Thunder rolled across the darkening sky. Tommy looked up.

Splat! Raindrops began to fall.

Tommy felt awful. This was the worstest day of his whole one-year-old life.

It would take a mighty powerful lizard to make everything right again.

Spike the dog dragged Angelica through the cattails along the stream. They passed the branch-canopied part of the river where the babies had played pirates not so long ago.

"I hope Cynthia 'preciates all my . . . love and demotion," she griped, spitting cattails out of her mouth.

Suddenly Spike sniffed the air and took off again.

"Stop!" Angelica shouted. "Spike, where are you going, you dumb dog?"

She ran after him, just as the gray wolf stuck its nose out of the bushes and sniffed Angelica's footprints.

All alone, Tommy trudged through the forest as a cold hard rain began to fall.

I gotta find my baby brother, he thought. *I just gotta!*

Wait. What was that? A high wailing noise coming through the rain. It sounded like a . . . Like a baby crying!

Tommy splashed through muddy puddles toward the sound. He peered through the rain and saw a horrible sight.

Two monkeys were dragging Baby Dil on a blanket!

"Hey!" Tommy shouted. "Gimme back my brother!" He ran toward the monkeys, waving his arms. "Shoo! Get out of here, you monkeys! Go!"

Startled, the monkeys let go of Dil and scampered away. Tommy heard them chattering angrily as they seemed to melt into the forest.

Dil smiled when he saw his big brother.

Tommy shook his head. He didn't think Dil had any idea how much trouble they were in. It was up to Tommy to keep them safe.

Tommy took his little brother by the hand. "C'mon, Dil. Let's get out of this rain."

Tommy found a large hole in a nearby tree and pulled Dil inside. Wet and exhausted, they huddled together, trying to keep warm.

Tommy had found his baby brother.

Would anybody find them?

Back at the ranger station, Frank and Margaret were watching the news on TV. Rex Pester was

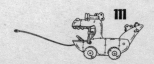

reporting from a helicopter hovering above the treetops.

Funny, Frank thought, leaning closer. *There's something familiar about that place. . . .*

CRASH! The door to the ranger station banged open. A strange shape stood outlined against the lightning.

"Dragons!" Frank complained. "There aren't supposed to be dragons out here! That's not in my contract."

But it wasn't a dragon. It was Didi Pickles and her friends. And she didn't have time to listen to this ranger rant and rave about mystical creatures right now.

Her babies were lost in the forest.

"Please," she begged the rangers. "Our kids are lost in the storm. You've got to help us!"

Frank wasn't sure she'd understood. "There are dragons out there! I'm a park ranger, not a Knight of the Round Table! Go find somebody with a lance!"

Margaret rolled her eyes and waved to Didi. "Never mind him," she said. "Come with me."

I hate storms! Tommy thought.

A flash of lightning made monster shadows dance among the gnarled trees. A slam of thunder made Tommy's heart thump.

But he tried to be brave—for Dil. "We'll just have a little bottle and take a nice nappie and everything'll be okay," he told his baby brother.

Tommy pulled a blanket out of the diaper bag—one of his old ones, his favorite. Tommy held the soft blanket to his face for a moment, breathing in the familiar smell. Then he wrapped it around him and his brother.

In the bottom of the diaper bag, he found the last full bottle.

"Mine! Mine!" Baby Dil chirped. He put the bottle in his mouth and began to drink.

"But I'm hungry, too," Tommy protested.

Dil sucked hungrily. Tommy grabbed the bottle and tried to pull it away, but Baby Dil held on with both hands and both feet.

"Dil, that's enough!" Tommy complained. "Stop it!" Didn't that baby store teach his brother anything about sharing?

SLURRRRP. Baby Dil drained the last of the milk, then let go of the bottle.

"You didn't save any for me!" Tommy exclaimed.

"All gone!" Baby Dil babbled. Then he pulled the soft warm blanket away from Tommy. "Mine."

Tommy was shocked. "Dil, I'm *cold!*" He pulled the blanket, but his brother wouldn't give an inch.

"My blankey! My blankey!" Dil argued.

Tommy shivered. "I need some blankey, too." He grabbed it and pulled hard.

Dil yanked back.

Riiiiip! An ugly jagged tear ripped down the middle of Tommy's favorite blanket.

Tommy fell back into a muddy puddle, and Dil laughed. Then the baby wrapped himself snugly in the torn blanket.

"Mokey!" Baby Dil giggled, pointing in Tommy's direction. "Mokey!"

That was the last straw for Tommy.

He'd tried. Really he had. He'd given up his crib without complaining. He'd given up most of his toys. He'd even lost his best friends in the world. And all because of Dil.

Being a big brother was just too hard.

"I don't got no more face in you!" Tommy yelled. "I'm through being your big brother. I don't wants my 'sponsitility no more!" He pulled the shiny watch from his diaper and threw it down in the mud.

He turned around to stomp off.

And came face to face with two monkeys.

The same two monkeys that had tried to kidnap Dil. They chittered and hopped excitedly outside the hollow tree. Dil spotted them and reached out his hand.

"Mokey! Mokey! My mokey! Mine!"

"Monkeys?" Tommy yelled. "Oh, okay, I'll give you monkeys!" He made a monkey face. He tried to copy the monkeys' sounds. "You'll have a monkey mommy and a monkey daddy and a monkey brother . . ."

As Tommy ranted and raved he dug feverishly through the diaper bag, tossing things left and right.

"I shoulda let my friends take you back to the hopsical. But 'No,' I said. 'He was only playin'.' Well, I was wrong. Now I don't even have friends!"

The monkeys began to pick through the stuff that Tommy threw on the ground.

Whack! Tommy tossed out Cynthia, Angelica's fashion doll, and it hit one of the monkeys on the forehead. The other monkey picked up the doll and examined it closely.

At last Tommy found what he was looking for. A jar of baby food. He popped open the top. The smell of banana rose in the damp air.

Dozens of monkeys flocked to the tree.

Tommy raised the open jar over Dil's bald little head.

"Mine!" Baby Dil shouted, reaching up for the jar. "My 'nanana! My 'nanana!"

"That's right," Tommy said. "Your nanners."

Tommy was going to dump the whole jar right on Dil's head. A giant glop of the gooey stuff gathered at the mouth of the jar. . . .

Suddenly a flash of lightning crashed, splitting open a nearby tree.

With a squeal, Baby Dil wrapped himself around his big brother, trembling in fear.

And that's when it happened.

All the mad feelings in Tommy's heart melted away.

The arms of his tiny baby brother clinging to him made him feel . . . good inside. As if he'd eaten a whole bag of chocolate coins.

Tommy looked down at his baby brother. Then at the baby food he was about to dump on Dil's tiny bald head.

Tommy dropped the jar.

"I'm sorry, Dil," he said. And he hugged his baby brother—really hugged him—for the very first time.

As more thunder rumbled above them, Tommy pulled Dil back into the hollow of the tree. Then he pulled the blanket up over the shivering child.

"It's okay, Dil," Tommy murmured. "Everything's gonna be okay."

He wasn't sure how. But somehow he was going to make that promise come true.

CHAPTER 11

Not far away, Phil and Lil toddled down a path with determination. Chuckie followed them, totally miserable. He was soaking wet. And he'd deserted the best friend he ever had.

Suddenly a bolt struck and splintered a huge dead tree.

It was going to fall right on top of them!

CRASH! The tree pounded onto the ground and lay still.

Then, out from the mud and branches popped a spiky red head smudged with dirt and bark—Chuckie!

He looked around. "Phil? Lil?"

The only sign of Phil was his muddy shoes,

sticking out from beneath the trunk of the fallen tree.

"Ahh!" Chuckie moaned. "Oh, Phil . . ."

"Chuckie?" Lil called out. She climbed out through some branches and toddled over. She spotted her twin brother's shoes and gasped.

"He always loved climbing on trees," Chuckie said, sniffling. "Now a tree's climbed on him."

Lil blinked back a tear. "He was my favoritest brother. Speak to me, Phillip!" she shouted at the shoes.

"Have you guys seen my shoes?" a voice behind them said.

Lil and Chuckie whirled around.

A barefoot Phil smiled at them from the other end of the tree.

"Phillip!" Lil squealed. She threw herself at him and hugged him tight. "I don't like this aventure anymore, Phillip."

Phil turned to Chuckie. "Gosh, Chuckie, this time we really are doomed."

"Doomed, doomed, doomed!" Lil chanted.

"Slap out of it, Lillian," Phil told his sister. "We gotta find the lizard."

"I don't know, guys," Chuckie said. "If we find the lizard and . . . and Tommy doesn't, how's he ever gonna get home?"

"What are you worried about *him* for?" Phil

wanted to know. "He's the one who was gonna let you get eated by a fish."

Lil crossed her arms. "All he cares about now is Baby Dil," she said with a look of disgust.

"Yeah, well, somebody has to," Chuckie shot back. "Don't they?"

Just then Tommy spotted something glinting in the mud—a gold watch. His 'sponsitility! Both covers were open, showing two pictures. One of Tommy and one of Dil.

"My Tomby," Baby Dil cooed when he saw the picture.

Tommy smiled and hugged his little brother. "My Dil."

Then he began to softly sing a lullaby to Dil.

Smiling at Dil, Tommy felt something blossom in his heart. Love for his brother.

He knew they probably wouldn't always get along. Dil would probably still drive him crazy sometimes.

But Tommy knew that from now on, they'd always be special to each other. Two brothers against the world!

And then the sound of chattering broke the peaceful silence.

The monkeys! Tommy looked out.

The tree was surrounded by monkeys. Hungry

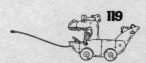

monkeys who smelled bananas.

The open jar of banana baby food sat in the mud a foot from Tommy's hand.

"Oh, uh, nice monkeys," Tommy said nervously. "You can have the nummy nanners now. Just leave us alone. Look . . ."

Uh-oh. The baby food jar was empty now. The yummy banana smell was coming from the baby food that Dil had splattered all over Tommy's and Dil's clothes.

As the monkeys closed in, Tommy tried desperately to wipe the food off. He tried to cover them with mud.

But the monkeys kept coming. They were determined. Hungry. And unstoppable.

Tommy wrapped his arms protectively around Dil, even as he trembled with fear.

The biggest monkey reached toward them with his claw–like hand.

"Not so fast, you monkeys!" Phil shouted. Phil and Lil had taken up positions on either side of Tommy and Dil's hollow tree.

"Phil!" Tommy cried. "And Lil! You came back! But where's—"

Pop! A strange sound rang through the forest. Like the sound a baby food jar makes when you pop open the airtight seal.

Tommy looked around.

His friend Chuckie stood in the clearing.

Chuckie was usually a chicken. A total fraidy-cat.

But not today. Today he faced down a pack of monkeys and stood his ground, defiantly holding up an open jar of banana baby food like a secret weapon.

"Chuckie!" Tommy yelled.

Chuckie waved. "Hi, Tommy!" he called. Then he turned to the monkeys and shouted, "Hey, monkeys! Want nanners? Well, come and get 'em!"

Chuckie turned and ran, carrying the banana food jar like a crazed Olympic torch bearer.

The monkeys ran after him.

"Gosh," Lil whispered, "I never knowed Chuckie was so brave."

"Yeah," said Phil. "I'm gonna miss him." He shrugged. "Well, we better get in the wagon and get outta here."

But Tommy heard another noise in the distance. One he recognized.

Now he had a plan.

He handed the still-sleeping Dil to Lil, secretly slipping something into Dil's diaper in the process.

"You guys take Dil and go look for the lizard," Tommy said solemnly. "I gotta go help my bestest friend."

• • •

Not far away, Spike dragged Angelica into a clearing in the woods. He charged ahead, sniffing excitedly.

"Dumb dog!" Angelica hollered. "There's no babies around here."

Crash!

At just that moment Chuckie streaked out of the woods and plowed into Angelica, sending her head over heels.

"Unnnh!" Angelica gasped as she landed flat on the ground, letting go of Spike's leash. "Chuckie?"

"Run, Angelica!" Chuckie yelled over his shoulder. "The monkeys is coming! The monkeys is coming!"

"Huh?" Angelica asked. Just as she rose to her knees—

Crash! A herd of monkeys ran over her and charged after Chuckie.

"Owff!" Angelica gasped. She picked herself up again, just in time to spot a little monkey bringing up the rear.

And it was carrying her Cynthia doll under its hairy little arm!

Angelica's eyes flashed. "Cynthia? Hey!" She tried to grab the doll, but the monkey scampered away.

With a shriek, Angelica ran after it.

No monkey was going to make a monkey out of her!

In the Pickleses' driveway, Grandpa Lou sat in the driver's seat of Stu's car with Chas beside him, holding a walkie-talkie.

A rope tied to the car's bumper led along the driveway, up the side of the garage, and across the roof to the peak where Stu sat. He was strapped into Dactar, his giant pterodactyl flying machine from the basement.

Stu pulled on an aerodynamic bicycle helmet that looked like a fin.

Chas radioed a final word of warning. "Be sure to watch out for the satellite dish."

"Don't worry," Stu said into his headset. "This time she'll fly! I'm facing into the wind!"

Stu knew his invention would come in handy one day.

And today was the day.

Flying through the sky, he'd find their babies in no time.

"He's ready?" Grandpa Lou asked Chas.

"No."

"Go?"

"No!"

"All righty, then!" Lou called merrily and stomped on the gas. The car jerked forward,

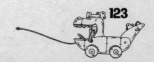

snapping the rope taut, hurling Stu into the air.

He yelled and dived, just missing several power lines.

"Arrgh!" Stu yelled. "Pop, cut me loose! Cut me loose!"

Chuckie was making a beeline through the woods toward a cliff he didn't know was there. The howling monkeys were right behind him.

When Chuckie saw the cliff, he went into a skid that ended inches from the perilous edge.

I guess this is the end of the road, Chuckie thought. He set down the baby food jar and turned to face the monkeys, who were emerging from the trees.

"Uh, nice monkeys, nice monkeys. I was only kiddin'," Chuckie said with a shaky grin. "Don't be mad at me. Please?"

The monkeys crept closer and closer.

Chuckie whimpered.

And then something wonderful happened.

Like Okeydokey Jones coming to the rescue, Tommy Pickles burst through the underbrush, riding Spike, both of his hands locked on the dog's collar.

Spike's barking frightened the monkeys, who skittered backward. Tommy reined in the dog and hopped off next to Chuckie.

"C'mon Chuckie!" Tommy said bravely. "We got a lizard to see!" He grabbed Chuckie's hand, and they tore out of there while Spike held the monkeys at bay.

A couple of monkeys got into a fight over the baby food. But the rest took off in angry pursuit!

Phil and Lil struggled to pull Dil in the Reptar Wagon.

Suddenly they heard a shout.

Tommy and Chuckie were headed straight for them.

But they had company.

Monkeys!

Phil and Lil left Dil in the wagon and rushed to help their friends.

But there were too many monkeys. They surrounded the babies. They started to drag Chuckie away.

Baby Dil, totally oblivious to all the danger, spotted something. It was the Reptar Wagon's brake handle. It was shiny and red and round.

"My ball!" Baby Dil cooed. He tugged hard on the handle. The Reptar Wagon began to roll.

Meanwhile, Tommy and his friends were losing their battle with the monkeys, even though Spike had joined them.

"Don't let 'em take me, Tommy!" Chuckie

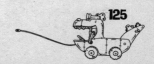

cried as the monkeys pulled him into a tree. "I don't wanna be a monkey boy!"

"Dil!" Tommy shouted. "C'mon you guys . . ."

Just as the monkeys were about to pull Chuckie into a tree—*STRIKE!* The Reptar Wagon bowled through the monkeys and kept going, now covered with babies. Chuckie fell from the tree and landed with a thud in the wagon. Spike chased a few more monkeys into the woods.

Not far away, Angelica had a tail-hold on the monkey who'd stolen her doll. He dragged her through the mud. He dragged her through a thorny bush. But Angelica wouldn't let go.

"Ow, ooh, ow, stop it!" Angelica yelled. It made her so mad, she bit his tail.

Yelping, the monkey dropped Cynthia. Angelica grabbed it and ran, wiping her tongue on her shirtsleeve to wipe the monkey taste from her mouth.

Just then the Reptar Wagon zipped by. And it was full of babies.

"Hey!" Angelica bellowed. "You stupid diaper bags! Wait for me!" But as she ran for the wagon, the little monkey jumped on her.

"Aaaagh!" Angelica yelled. "I've got a monkey on my back!"

Angelica jumped onto Reptar's tail and started

to climb into the wagon, trying to pry off the monkey.

"Nah nah nah nah nah! Dumb monkeys!"

Clank! Suddenly the wagon dropped onto the railroad tracks and started for the old trestle bridge like a runaway train. The force of the fall knocked Angelica from Reptar's tail, and she was dragged behind the wagon on her rear end.

"OOH! OW! OOH! OW! OOH! OW!" Angelica hollered as she bounced over the rails.

But at least it bumped the monkey off her.

The babies didn't even know she was there as they zoomed across the old wooden bridge spanning the river.

In the distance they spotted a cabin. The ranger station.

But to the babies it looked like a house from a fairy tale. A house where a wizard might live.

"Look!" Chuckie cried. "The lizard's house!"

The babies cheered. It looked as if their problems were over at last.

Angelica at last managed to crawl into the wagon. "After all I've done for you babies, you were gonna leave me and Cynthia behinnnnnnnnnd—"

Crunch! Halfway across the bridge, a rotten plank gave way. The wagon lurched to a stop, balancing over the hole.

Angelica flew out the front of the wagon.

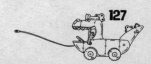

Phil was surprised. "I didn't know she could fly."

"I think it's because she's a witch!" Lil said.

Angelica hung on to Reptar, dangling precariously above the swollen river. Below her, the water rushed wildly toward the roaring falls. Behind her, the monkeys started onto the bridge.

"Hang on, Angelica!" Tommy shouted. He and the others struggled to pull her up.

Didi, Betty, Charlotte, and Drew rode through the forest in the ranger's Jeep.

"Oh, we'll never find them," Didi worried, wringing her hands. "Can't you do something?"

"C'mon, baby!" Margaret said to the Jeep as they struggled over the rough roads. "C'mon!"

Over the radio came a cracked voice. Stu!

"Sky Pickle to Ground Pickle," the voice said.

"Stu!" Didi cried.

Drew rolled his eyes and whispered to his wife Charlotte. "What's that numbskull up to now?"

But when Didi looked up into the sky, she saw a beautiful sight. A soaring pterodactyl flying machine! A guy in a bicycle helmet was pedaling like mad to keep it aloft.

"Stu!" Didi shouted. "Is that you?"

"Roger that," Stu said into his headset. "We have aerial search!"

A flock of geese interrupted his report.

"Whoaaaaaaaa!" Stu yelled. He couldn't see a thing through all the feathers. But he had to keep pedaling, or he'd fall to the ground.

Not far away another flying machine was circling the same area. It was Rex Pester reporting from the Action News helicopter. And once again he was really mixing up the facts. "A truckload of babies and their pet horse, lost in the woods. Our hearts go out to . . ."

Crash! Dactar's head ripped through the windshield, just missing Rex. Stu was practically inside the cockpit now.

Rex Pester was horrified. "You! What are you doing in here? Get out!" he yelled. He kicked at Stu and shoved him out of the cockpit.

"AHHHHHHHHHHH!" Stu yelled.

Dactar broke loose from the helicopter.

Both flying vehicles went into a spin.

They were going to crash!

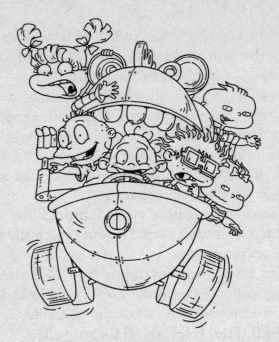

CHAPTER 12

Down at the railroad trestle the bridge creaked and groaned as the babies finally pulled Angelica back into the Reptar Wagon.

But the monkeys were nearly upon them.

Chuckie covered his spikey red head. "Don't let 'em take me!" he cried.

"Don't let 'em take Cynthia!" Angelica shouted to anyone who would listen.

"I don't think they're gonna take anyone," Lil told them. "Look."

To everyone's surprise, the monkeys stopped, chattered wildly, then turned and raced back into the woods.

"Yippee!" the kids cheered.

But their celebration was cut short by the horrible growl. The babies turned around to see a snarling gray wolf at the other end of the bridge, blocking their path to the ranger station. The creature growled and licked his chops as he started toward the children.

Chuckie looked longingly toward the lizard's house. They were so close! Maybe it would still work if they made a wish pretty close to the lizard.

"We wanna go home," Chuckie began to chant. "We wanna go home!"

The wolf lunged.

Suddenly a heroic bark rang out! Spike leaped over the wagon, colliding with the wolf in midair.

"Spike!" Tommy shouted.

"Get him, Spike!" Phil and Lil shouted.

"Be careful," Chuckie reminded him.

The wolf growled and snapped at Spike. Spike leaped to avoid his jaws, but soon both animals were a blur of fur and teeth.

The babies shouted and yelled for Spike.

Baby Dil clapped and giggled. He thought the beasts were playing.

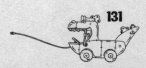

But the wolf was too strong for Spike. He was almost licked.

In his final effort to save the babies, the loyal dog sank his teeth into the wolf's hind leg and backed off the bridge, pulling the bigger animal with him.

In an instant, they disappeared over the side.

The babies heard a splash far below.

"'pike?" Dil cooed, confused.

But Spike was gone.

Tommy picked up Spike's torn collar from the bridge. He'd known the dog his whole life. He couldn't believe he was gone.

"Oh, Spike," he whispered as he looked over the edge.

"Dumb dog," Angelica muttered, then sniffed back a tear. She didn't really mean it. She'd actually begun to sorta like the mutt.

None of them would ever forget how he had given his life to save them from the jaws of the gray wolf.

High overhead Stu pulled the Dactar out of a dive just in time to spot some kids on the bridge.

Their kids!

"Deed!" he shouted into his headset. "I found them! They're over by the ranger station! I'm goin' iiiinnn . . ."

The Dactar flying machine dropped like a stone and crashed through the roof of a toolshed.

Tommy and his friends spun around just in time to see the walls of the old building collapse.

In the middle of the rubble Stu Pickles sat draped in Dactar's wings. The bicycle helmet had slipped down over his face, with the pointed end straight up.

Dizzy from his crash, Stu slowly rose to his feet.

Tommy gasped. He didn't know it was his dad.

To the babies, he looked like some tall mythical creature who lived in the woods.

"The lizard!" the kids cried in awe.

The lizard was scarier than Tommy had ever imagined. But they needed his help. Someone *had* to ask.

I'll do it, Tommy thought bravely. *I'll face the lizard—for Dil and all my friends.*

Tommy stepped forward, holding Spike's collar. He swallowed, then made their one wish.

"Please, Mr. Lizard," Tommy said. "We wish we could go—"

Tommy choked. He was supposed to say "We wish we could go home." But he couldn't.

They had only one wish. And Tommy knew what it had to be. "We wish we had our doggie back!"

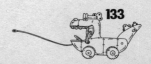

Like magic, Stu's battered radio erupted in sparks. A cloud of smoke billowed from his helmet. He groaned as a sudden gust of wind caught his dinosaur wings, whisking him toward the ravine.

Down he tumbled, crashing and rolling, till he came to the bottom of the ravine. When he came to a stop, a dog was in his arms.

It was Spike! The doggie jumped out of Stu's arms and barked happily.

Tommy couldn't believe his eyes. Spike was alive. He was all right!

The power of the lizard's magic filled Tommy Pickles with wonder.

Moments later Ranger Margaret skidded her Jeep to a stop nearby.

Didi Pickles flew from the car.

Their nightmare was over. They'd found the babies!

She scooped her two boys into her arms.

"Oh, Dil!" Didi cried, covering them with kisses. "My Tommy!"

Tommy hugged his mom as if he'd never let go.

Everything was going to be all right.

He had taken good care of his baby brother. He was proud of himself for that.

But he was only one year old, after all. Now he

was ready to let his mom and dad take care of him for a while.

Betty and Howard both picked up a twin to hug. Then they traded, and the hugging started all over again.

Chas scooped up Chuckie and spun him around in the air.

Angelica threw herself into her mom and dad's arms. They were so lucky to have her back!

Spike ran circles around them all, barking his approval.

But the families' private reunion was soon interrupted by the outside world.

Reporters surrounded the smiling families. Lights from news vans and police cars lit up the woods. Television cameras recorded every detail.

Flash! A news photographer took a group picture. The babies and their parents looked tired. And dirty.

And very, very happy.

When the picture ran in the newspaper, the caption underneath said "Reptar Saves the Day."

Tommy and his friends were famous. People from all over found out about their big adventures.

Tommy's dad won that big toy contest and never did have to get a real job. He even got to go to Japan and meet Mr. Yamaguchi.

135

As time went by, Dil seemed not to cry quite so much. And he followed his big brother Tommy wherever he went.

Didi made sure to hug her children more often. And when she read Tommy his bedtime stories, she always made it through to the very last page.

After a while, things settled down to normal.

But Tommy's world was never the same again.

And he was glad.

Thanks to his new brother, Dil, it was even better.

Once again the babies found themselves in the temple, bathed in eerie white light. Before a high, cold altar they formed a pyramid, attempting to capture the golden object.

Only *this* time there was one more baby to help.

Tommy held Dil high above them, and Dil was able to reach the large golden treasure.

Everyone cheered!

About the Authors

Cathy East Dubowski and Mark Dubowski started writing and illustrating children's books while they lived in a small apartment in New York City. Now they work in two old barns on Morgan Creek near Chapel Hill, North Carolina. They live with their daughters, Lauren and Megan, and a golden retriever named Macdougal.

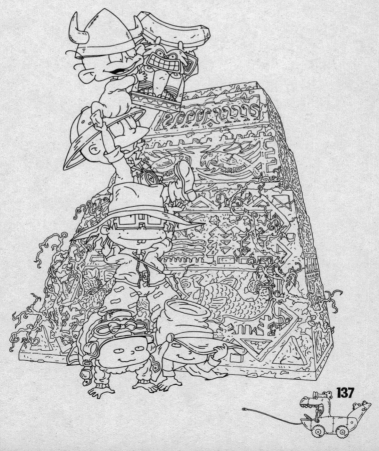